The Kid's Microwave Cookbook

by Sally Murphy Morris
illustrated by Kathleen Patterson-Estes

BRISTOL PUBLISHING ENTERPRISES, INC.
San Leandro, California

A Nitty Gritty® Cookbook

©1991 Bristol Publishing Enterprises, Inc. P.O. Box 1737, San Leandro, California 94577. World rights reserved. No part of this publication may be reproduced by any mechanical, photographic, or electronic process, or in the form of a phonographic recording, nor may it be stored in a retrieval system, transmitted, or otherwise copied for public or private use without prior written permission from the publisher.

Printed in the United States of America.

ISBN 1-55867-018-1

Contents

HOT DRINKS	12
BREAKFAST	19
FRUITS	30
THE MAIN COURSE	41
CASSEROLES	53
VEGGIES	68
DESSERTS	85
SNACKS AND MINI MEALS	102
CANDY	119

A Note To Parents:

Boys and girls of all ages love to eat. And they love to take care of this need to feed themselves. When you teach them to cook, they will have a skill for a lifetime.

Before they begin, be sure your children understand how the microwave oven operates. The first step is to go over the manual that comes with the oven. Make certain they know which utensils are acceptable for use (glass, ceramic, specially designed plastics). Remind them that metal and metal-trimmed objects cannot be used. You may want to gather acceptable cookware in one spot for ease of use, or mark acceptable pieces with a permanent pen. Younger cooks must understand how to read and follow the recipe, how to use equipment properly, how to measure, how to handle food, and how to clean up afterwards. Start with very easy recipes with few ingredients. When they are mastered, more difficult recipes can be tried.

All foods are not successfully prepared in the microwave. The best are fruits, vegetables, fish, poultry, casseroles, and some desserts. Foods that require a dry heat to crisp or brown such as cookies, some cakes, and most breads will not do well. Nor will foods such as angel food cakes and soufflés. For popcorn, use only a microwave corn popper or the specially formulated bags of corn, which cannot be reused.

   These recipes are the foods kids most love to eat. In the microwave they cook quickly and will retain more color, texture and flavor than with other cooking methods. They range from high calorie snacks to be eaten occasionally to nutritious family dinners for daily use. They are kitchen tested and easy to prepare. They were tested in 650 and 700 watt ovens. If yours has less wattage, slightly longer cooking times may be needed. See page 10 for *Equivalents in Microwave Times.*

Safety Tips

- Younger cooks can begin by closing the oven door, pushing the buttons, and stirring. When they are older they can be given greater responsibility. It is a good idea to position the oven at their level so that they don't have to balance on a chair or ladder, but never should faces be closer than 12 inches to the oven door.

- Keep hot pads handy. The foods in the oven get hot, and hot food can burn.

- When using processed food, follow package directions carefully.

- If food has been covered, the containers should always be opened away from the face to prevent accidents from hot steam. The hands should be protected from steam burns.

- When using plastic wrap as a cover, use over a deep dish, and leave one corner uncovered for steam to escape. This is called venting.

- Dense foods (soup, stew, casseroles, pudding) should be stirred for even heating.

- For ovens without a turntable, rearrange foods such as potatoes, squash and apples. These foods should be pierced before cooking to prevent explosions.

- Rotate foods such as pizza, brownies, and baked items for even cooking if you do not have a turntable. This means turning the item 1/4 or 1/2 turn clockwise several times.

- Never leave the kitchen while food is in the oven. It needs to be monitored.

- Never microwave eggs in their shell. They explode, and make a terrible mess. I don't recommend cooking them in any manner in the microwave except well mixed and scrambled, as the membrane surrounding them acts like a balloon unless it has been pierced, and is still apt to explode.

- Do not heat food in a narrow-necked bottle, as the bottle can shatter.

- Microwave browning dishes are not recommended for use by children as they can reach temperatures over 750° during preheating.

- Use only microwave-safe plastic wrap. Plastic storage bags are not formulated for oven use and can disintegrate with heat.

- Do not use metal, styrofoam, waxed containers, recycled paper and plastic not designated for the microwave.

- Do not put hot containers on or near plastic or synthetic tableclothes.

- Never operate the oven empty. It will damage or shorten the life of the magnetron.

- For mixtures with milk, use a container 2 to 3 times larger than the quantity you are cooking to avoid boil-overs.

Safety Test

- To be sure a mug, bowl or casserole is safe to use in a microwave oven, fill a glass measuring cup (such as Pyrex or Fire King) with water. Put it and the piece you are testing in the microwave. Microwave on HIGH 1 minute. The water in the cup should feel warm, but the empty container should not. If it is cool, it is safe.

A Note to Kids:

Do you love to eat? Silly question. Everybody loves to eat. But did you know eating is even more fun when you have prepared the food yourself? It is easy and fast when you use the microwave oven to do your cooking. But remember, a microwave is not a toy. You must be careful with the microwave, and the food that comes from it, for your health and safety.

- At first you need to work with a parent or other adult to be sure you know how the oven operates.
- When you are ready to begin cooking, find the recipe you want to make. Read it carefully to be certain you understand the words in it.
- Ask for permission to cook.
- Check to see if you have all the ingredients you will need.
- Ask which pans are safe in the microwave.

- Wash your hands.

- Just to be sure, read through the directions again.

- Get out the dishes, measuring utensils and ingredients you will need.

- Get out the hot pads, too. Hot food can transfer heat to the dish you are cooking in. You won't enjoy your food if you have been burned.

It is very important to use the correct container. Glass works best, and the recipes here specify it, but sometimes you can use paper, certain plastics made for the microwave, and ceramic materials such as Corningware and glazed pottery. Again, ask an adult about this.

Never use any metal in the oven. If it should spark, you will get a terrible scare and your oven could be damaged. Since microwaves won't pass through metal, your food will not get cooked.

It is fun to watch baked goods rise, and it is necessary to watch to see when cheese is melted, but *KEEP YOUR EYES AWAY FROM THE MICROWAVE OVEN*

DOOR. It is an excellent rule to stay at least 12 inches from the oven when it is on. Protect yourself!

It is also important to clean up the kitchen when you finish. This can often be done while the food is cooking. Sponge off the counters, wash and dry the dishes, and put them away. Cleaning up is as important as cooking.

For Beginners

Look for this B next to a recipe. It is a good choice for you if you are a beginner. But even if you are a good cook already, you will want to try it!

How the Microwave Oven Operates

Most questions about a microwave oven can be answered in the use and care booklet that came with your oven. It explains the features of your oven.

The microwave oven is an enclosed metal box with a power source called the *magnetron tube*. When the oven is turned on, the tube sends out very short radio waves. These are directed by either an antenna or a fan blade, which directs them to the walls of the oven. The waves will not pass through metal, but are reflected by it to the food. When they reach the food they act upon the water molecules in it, setting them in motion. The rapidly moving molecules cause friction, which produces heat, which cooks the food. The food gets hot but the air surrounding it does not. However, the heat in the food can transfer to the cooking container, causing it to get warm.

Ovens vary in the amount of power they put out (called *watts*), and this in turn affects the cooking time. Recipes in this book were tested in 650 and 700 watt ovens. A sticker on the door and your use and care book will tell you what yours has. If it is less, you will need to add more time to the time listed for the recipes in this book. See page 10 for *Equivalents in Microwave Times.*

Always undercook food. You can add another 30 seconds or more of cooking time, but if you overcook food and it becomes hard there is little you can do except start over. As you try recipes, make notes on the timing in the margin. The next time, your timing will be just right for your microwave oven.

Equivalents in Microwave Times

600 to 750 watts	**500 to 600 watts**	**400 to 500 watts**
15 seconds	18 seconds	20 seconds
30 seconds	35 seconds	45 seconds
1 minute	1 minute 15 seconds	1 minute 30 seconds
2 minutes	2 minutes 30 seconds	2 minutes 50 seconds
3 minutes	3 minutes 30 seconds	4 minutes 15 seconds
4 minutes	4 minutes 50 seconds	5 minutes 45 seconds
5 minutes	6 minutes	7 minutes
10 minutes	12 minutes	14 minutes

Glossary of Important Terms

cooking time: power level and time needed for the oven to operate. Timing is affected by: starting temperature; moisture, fat and sugar content; quantity; size, shape and density of food; arrangement; covers; oven wattage

glass measure: measuring cups in various sizes with useful handles

magnetron tube: the power source for the short wave radio waves

microwave safe: means microwaves can pass through to cook the food. See Safety Test, page 5.

rearrange: move the portion on the outside in and the inside out for even cooking

rotate or turn: move the food 1/4 or 1/2 turn clockwise several times for even cooking. Not necessary with a turntable.

standing or resting time: the time after the oven is off when the temperature in the food equalizes itself and the cooking process is completed

stir: mix to help casseroles and other dense foods cook evenly

vent: after covering a dish with microwave-safe plastic wrap, turn back one corner to allow a small amount of steam to escape

Hot Drinks

Hot drinks are comforting, filling, and a welcome change from soft drinks. Best of all, they are very easy to make, requiring nothing more than a measuring spoon, a few ingredients, and a microwave-safe cup or mug.

Old Fashioned Cocoa 13
Nanny's Cocoa Mix 14
Cocoa from a Mix. 14
Hot Lemon Tea 15
Orange Spiced Tea 16
Hot Vegetable Cocktail. . . 17
Spiced Cider 18

Old Fashioned Cocoa

You can skip the marshmallows, but they taste so good when melted by the hot cocoa.

1 heaping tbs. cocoa mix (containing sugar)
  or use 1½ tsp. unsweetened ground cocoa and 1½ tsp. sugar
¾ cup milk
2 large or 6 small marshmallows

Put cocoa mix in a glass mug, or one made of ceramic or heavy plastic. Pour in a little milk. Stir until smooth. Add remaining milk. Microwave on **HIGH** 1½ minutes. Never let milk boil or it will expand and go over the top. Top with marshmallows and let the hot cocoa melt them, or return the mug to the oven and heat on **HIGH** 10 to 20 seconds. Makes 1 serving.

HOT DRINKS

Nanny's Cocoa Mix

This low-priced recipe makes a huge batch. Store in a container with a tight lid.

1 pkg. (8 qt.) instant dry milk
1 jar (11 oz.) powdered cream
2 lb. can instant chocolate drink mix
½ cup powdered sugar

In a large bowl, mix the ingredients until blended. Store in a 5-quart container. Makes up to 125 servings.

Cocoa from a Mix

¾ cup water
⅓ cup Nanny's cocoa mix

Measure water into a microwave-safe mug. Microwave on **HIGH** 1½ to 2 minutes. Add mix and stir well. Makes 1 serving.

Hot Lemon Tea

Hot lemon tea warms you up on a chilly day.

3/4 cup water
1 tsp. presweetened instant tea mix with lemon

Measure water into a microwave-safe mug. Microwave on **HIGH** 1½ to 2 minutes. Stir in the tea mix. Wait until it cools a bit before drinking. Makes 1 serving.

Orange Spiced Tea

You can taste tangy, sweet and spicy flavors.

2 cups orange-flavored drink mix
2 cups sugar
½ cup instant tea without sugar
1 tsp. cinnamon
½ tsp. ground cloves

Combine ingredients and stir well. Store in a 1½ quart container with a tight lid. Makes 40-45 servings.

Individual Serving

¾ cup water
1½ tsp. orange spiced tea mix

Measure water into a microwave-safe mug. Microwave on **HIGH** 1½ to 2 minutes. Stir in the tea mix. Makes 1 serving.

Hot Vegetable Cocktail

*This recipe has a **savory** flavor. What does savory mean?*

1 can (12 oz.) vegetable juice cocktail
1 tsp. lemon juice
½ tsp. Worcestershire sauce

In a 4-cup glass measure, mix all ingredients together. Microwave on **HIGH** 4 to 6 minutes, uncovered. Makes 2 servings.

Spiced Cider

This delicious drink tastes like fall!

¾ cup (6 oz.) apple cider or apple juice
1 tsp. brown sugar
1 cinnamon stick

Heat cider or juice and brown sugar in a microwave-safe mug on **HIGH** 1½ to 2 minutes. Use a cinnamon stick to stir a few times. Drop it in the mug, but don't try to eat the stick. Makes 1 serving.

Heating Times

1 mug liquid	**HIGH**	1½ to 2 minutes
2 mugs liquid	**HIGH**	2 to 2½ minutes
3 mugs liquid	**HIGH**	3 to 3½ minutes

Breakfast

The best thing you can do for yourself is to start the day with a good breakfast. Good nutrition gives you "go power" all day long. For variety, try one of the easy ideas here. It really is fun when you have made it yourself.

Scrambled Eggs 20
Green Eggs and Ham 21
Bacon 22
Huevos Rancheros 23
Blueberry Coffee Cake . . . 24
Old-Fashioned Oatmeal . 25
Quick Oatmeal 25
Refrigerator Bran Muffins . . 26
Quick Muffins 28

Scrambled Eggs

Eggs cook in a hurry, but you have to stir them so they'll cook evenly.

2 tsp. margarine or butter
4 eggs
4 tbs. water

Put margarine in a 1-quart casserole. Microwave on **HIGH** 45 to 60 seconds until margarine is melted. Break eggs into the same dish. Using a fork, pierce the yolks and mix up the eggs a little bit. Add water and stir until the eggs are well mixed. Microwave on **HIGH** for 2 minutes. Stir well, bringing the cooked edges toward the middle. Microwave on **HIGH** 2 to 3 minutes, stirring after each minute until nearly set. Allow to stand, covered, to complete cooking and firm up. Makes 2 to 4 servings.

A Good Idea

A few tablespoons of meat cubes and some grated cheese make these special. You can also add some chopped green pepper or green onion. Yum!

Green Eggs and Ham

This recipe from Dr. Seuss is good for a party or a super-silly supper.

4 eggs
1/4 cup water
1/4 tsp. salt
blue food coloring
1/2 cup chopped ham
4 tsp. butter or margarine

Break eggs into a jar with a tight lid. Add milk and salt. Put the lid on and shake well. Add blue food coloring, one drop at a time. Cover and shake after each drop. When a "lovely" green color is reached, stop. Add the ham.

In a small casserole, microwave butter on **HIGH** 30 to 45 seconds until it melts. Add the eggs. Microwave on **HIGH** 3 to 4 minutes, stirring often after the first minute. When just set, remove the casserole from the microwave and put it on a heat-proof surface. Let it stand until the eggs are firm. Makes 2 to 4 servings.

Bacon

The paper towels soak up the fat and stop the spatters.

4 slices bacon

Find a glass pan about 8 inches wide and 11 inches long. Line it with 3 layers of paper towels. Peel the bacon apart and place the pieces in the pan, side by side. Put another paper towel on top. Microwave on HIGH 3½ to 6 minutes, depending on how thick the bacon is. It should be nearly crisp. Remove the top towel and let the bacon stand a few minutes to crisp and cool slightly. Makes 2 servings.

Huevos Rancheros

Say it: hoo-way-vose ran-chair-ose. If you can't pronounce it, you can still cook it, and call it **Eggs in a Blanket.** *What a fun change from the usual breakfast! Olé!*

1 tsp. margarine or butter
1 egg
1 tsp. water

1 flour tortilla
salsa or taco sauce
1 tbs. grated cheese

Put butter in a 1-cup glass measuring cup. Microwave on **MEDIUM** (50%) 45 to 60 seconds. Break eggs into melted margarine. Add water. Beat with a fork. Microwave on **MEDIUM** (50%) 30 to 45 seconds. Stir well. Microwave on **MEDIUM** (50%) about 30 seconds more. Remove from oven. Cover with plastic wrap and let stand 1 minute.

Meanwhile, wrap the tortilla in a kitchen towel or a paper towel. Microwave on **HIGH** 15 seconds to soften. Put the tortilla on a plate, spoon the egg down the middle, and add salsa or taco sauce and cheese. Roll up the tortilla and put the seam side down on a plate. To eat it, pick it up in your hands like a hot dog. Makes 1 serving.

Deluxe Version: Add chopped green onions and diced tomatoes with the cheese. Top with sour cream and guacamole (avocado dip) if you like them.

Blueberry Coffee Cake

This is really easy, because most of the measuring is already done.

1 pkg. (13 oz.) blueberry muffin mix
2 tbs. brown sugar
½ tsp. cinnamon
2 tbs. soft butter or margarine

Follow the muffin mix directions on the side of the package. Find a 9-inch round glass or plastic cake dish, and pour the mix into it. Microwave on **HIGH** 5½ to 6½ minutes until the top is just dry. Rotate after 3 minutes if your oven does not have a turntable.

While the cake is baking, mix the brown sugar and cinnamon in a small bowl. When the cake is done, brush with soft butter. Sprinkle the cinnamon mix on top. Let the cake stand on a heat-proof surface about 10 minutes before cutting. Makes 8 servings.

Old Fashioned Oatmeal

1/3 cup old fashioned rolled oats

3/4 cup water

Combine oats and water in a large (16 oz.) microwave-safe bowl. Microwave on **MEDIUM** (50%) 4½ to 6 minutes until thickened. Stir. Let the oatmeal stand a few minutes before eating it. Makes 1 serving.

Quick Oatmeal

1/3 cup instant oatmeal or 1 pkg. (1 oz.) instant oatmeal
2/3 cup water

Combine oats and water in a large (16 oz.) microwave-safe cereal bowl. Microwave on **HIGH** about 1½ minutes. Stir. Let the oatmeal stand 1 minute before eating. Makes 1 serving.

Some Good Ideas

Before cooking, add any of the following: ½ apple, chopped; 1 tbs. raisins; 1 tbs. any dried fruit; ½ tsp. cinnamon.

After cooking, add any of the following: butter and brown sugar; 2 tbs. applesauce; ¼ cup mini marshmallows; 1½ tbs. maple syrup; chopped nuts; your favorite chips.

Refrigerator Bran Muffins

If you have the batter in your refrigerator you can have a hot treat in minutes. If you bake with 2 paper muffin cup liners, you will bake a better muffin.

1 cup hot water
1 cup Nabisco 100% Bran cereal
2 cups Kellog's All Bran cereal
2 cups buttermilk
1½ cups sugar

2 eggs
½ cup oil
2½ cups flour
2½ tsp. baking soda
½ tsp. salt

Measure water into a 1-cup glass measuring cup. Microwave on **HIGH** 2½ minutes. Meanwhile, measure cereals into a large bowl with a cover. Pour the hot water over the cereals. Stir in the other ingredients in the order they are listed. Just stir a little bit, until the ingredients are mixed.

Then line a microwave muffin pan or six custard cups with 2 layers of paper liners. Fill cups half full, being careful not to stir the batter any more as you spoon it out. Arrange the custard cups in a circle in your oven. Microwave on **HIGH** 3 minutes for a muffin pan, and about 6 minutes for custard cups.

When the muffins are nearly dry on top, take them out of the oven. Remove the muffins from the cups and let them stand a few minutes. They are the best if you eat them soon after you make them. Leftover batter can be kept in the refrigerator for 2 or 3 weeks. Makes 36 muffins.

Muffin Timings

To *cook*, microwave on **HIGH**		To *reheat frozen*, microwave on **HIGH**	
1 muffin	30 to 45 seconds	1 muffin	15 to 20 seconds
2 muffins	45 to 60 seconds	2 muffins	30 to 40 seconds
3 muffins	60 to 90 seconds	3 muffins	40 to 60 seconds

Quick Muffins

You can have muffins in less than 15 minutes. With several fruit choices, you can make a different kind every time.

1/4 cup chopped pecans, walnuts, or bran cereal
1 tbs. brown sugar
1/2 tsp. cinnamon
1 cup flour
3 tbs. sugar
1 1/2 tsp. baking powder
1/2 tsp. salt

1 tsp. cinnamon
1 egg
1/2 cup milk
2 tbs. vegetable oil
1/2 cup fruit
   (a peeled apple, finely chopped, or blueberries, or raspberries, or raisins are good)

Line a microwave muffin pan or six custard cups with 2 paper liners for each muffin. In a small bowl, mix nuts, brown sugar and cinnamon. This will be your topping. Put it to one side.

In a medium bowl, stir flour with sugar, baking powder, salt and cinnamon. In a small bowl, beat the egg with a fork. Add milk, oil and fruit to the egg. Add all of this wet mixture to the flour, and stir just a little bit, until you see no dry parts. Do not stir too much!

Spoon the batter into the muffin cups. Put a spoonful of topping on each muffin. Microwave on **HIGH** 3 to 3½ minutes until the muffins are almost dry on top. If you do not have a turntable, rotate the muffins clockwise ¼ turn after every minute. Push a toothpick into the center of a muffin. If it comes out clean, the muffins are ready to take out of the oven. Let them sit a few minutes before serving. Makes 6 large muffins.

About the Muffin Pan

A microwave muffin pan with cups arranged in a circle is good to have. Or cut the top 1 inch off six 6- or 7-ounce styrofoam, plastic or paper hot drink cups. Arrange the top rings on a flat plate in a circle. Or use 6-ounce custard cups. Put 2 paper liners in each cup for best results. Rotate the whole plate ¼ turn clockwise several times during cooking.

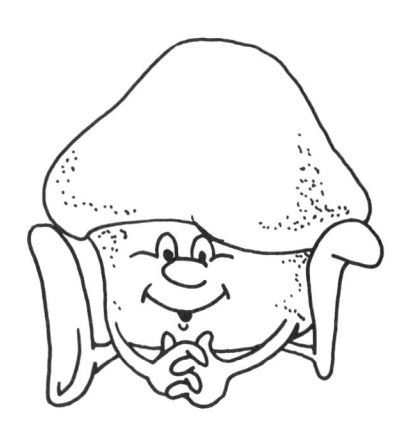

Fruits

Fruits are perfect for the microwave. They are sweet and packed with goodness. They cook in a hurry and don't need many other ingredients to make them taste good. They're good for you, and interesting, so enjoy them often.

Frozen Banana Pops. . . .	31
Appleberry Salad	32
Baked Apples	33
Poached Pears	34
Peach Cobbler.	35
Applesauce.	36
Strawberry Pretzel Dessert	38
Pear Crisp	40

Frozen Banana Pops

This snack is fun to make and healthy too.

1 pkg. (6 oz.) chocolate chips
¼ cup milk
4 or 5 bananas
8 to 10 popsicle sticks

1 cup topping, such as rice krispies, granola, chopped peanuts, or coconut

Cover two plates with waxed paper. Place chips and milk in a small microwave-safe bowl. Microwave on **MEDIUM** (50%) 2 to 3 minutes until chocolate has melted. Stir hard after 2 minutes. Continue to cook if necessary. Stir until smooth.

Peel the bananas and cut each in half. Insert a stick into each half, beginning at the cut end. Put the topping on one plate. Dip each banana in chocolate and immediately roll it in the topping. Put it on the second plate. When all of the bananas are coated, put them in the freezer to firm up for about 20 minutes. Eat immediately or save for another day. Makes 4 to 5 servings.

Appleberry Salad

Make this salad a few hours before serving, so it has time to become firm.

1 cup water
1 pkg. (3 oz.) raspberry or strawberry gelatin
2 cups applesauce
4 lettuce leaves

In a 4-cup glass measuring cup, microwave water on **HIGH** 3 minutes, until boiling. Carefully add gelatin, and stir to completely dissolve. Refrigerate until slightly thickened, about 2 hours. Stir in applesauce. Pour into 4 glass custard cups, a salad mold, or an 8 by 8-inch square pan. Chill until firm, several hours.

To unmold individual servings, pour warm water into a pan. Carefully dip mold about ½ inch into water for no more than 10 seconds. Put lettuce leaves on small plates, and turn the custard cups over on the lettuce leaves. For a square pan, cut in 4 equal pieces and remove with a spatula. Makes 4 servings.

Baked Apples

Baked apples smell so good as they cook you will have everyone waiting to eat them.

4 large crisp apples
4 tsp. brown sugar

cinnamon
¼ cup orange or apple juice, or water

Wash and core each apple. Peel a 1-inch band of skin from the top half. Place each apple in a 6-ounce baking cup or put them all in a round glass cake dish. Measure 1 teaspoon of brown sugar into the hole in each and sprinkle with cinnamon. Add 1 tablespoon of juice to each. Arrange in a circle in the oven. Microwave on **HIGH** 8 to 10 minutes until apples are soft. Serve with cream if you like it. Makes 4 servings.

For 1 baked apple: follow directions, but microwave on **HIGH** 4 to 5 minutes.

Some Good Ideas

Put a few raisins in the hole, or use 2 large or 8 miniature marshmallows in each hole in place of the cinnamon and sugar.

Poached Pears

"Poach" means cook in liquid. The fruit juice gives a different flavor to mild pears. Next time, don't use the cinnamon and try pineapple juice. Top with crushed berries. Yum!

¼ cup red cinnamon candies
1 cup apple cider or apple juice
2 large ripe pears
Custard Sauce, page 101
2 macaroon cookies, crumbled, if you like them

Place candies in a 1-quart casserole. Add cider or juice. Microwave on **HIGH** about 5 minutes, until candies are melted. Stir. Peel the pears and cut them in half. Remove the cores. Place them cut side down in the juice-candy syrup. Cover. Microwave on **HIGH** about 6 minutes, until the pears are tender. Chill.

To serve, place each pear half in a dessert dish, cut side up. Spoon some sauce on top of each pear, and then some custard sauce and cookie crumbs. Makes 4 servings.

Peach Cobbler

Cobbler is really good with ice cream or frozen yogurt.

4 peaches, peeled and sliced
1 tsp. cinnamon
3 tbs. sugar
¼ cup butter or margarine
1 pkg. (9½ oz.) 1-layer cake mix or ½ of a 2-layer mix

Arrange peach slices in an 8-inch square pan or a 9-inch Corningware skillet. Mix cinnamon and sugar together, and sprinkle it over peaches. Microwave on **HIGH** 3 minutes. In a glass bowl or a 4-cup glass measuring cup, melt the butter on **MEDIUM HIGH** (70%) about 2 minutes. Add the cake mix and stir until crumbly. Use your hands if you want to. Crumble the cake mix over the peaches.
   Microwave on **HIGH** about 10 minutes, turning the dish ¼ turn every 2 minutes if you do not have a turntable. Cool slightly. Serve with ice cream, whipped cream, or frozen yogurt. Makes 6 to 8 servings.

Applesauce

If you have an apple tree or know someone who does, you can make many batches of applesauce in no time. It's good on hot cereal, pancakes, gingerbread, and pork roast.

1½ lbs. cooking apples (Granny Smith, Gravenstein,
  Golden Delicious or Pippins are good)
¼ cup water
3 to 4 sticks of cinnamon

Core apples but do not peel. Cut each apple in 8 pieces. Put them in a 2½ or 3-quart casserole with a lid. Fill it to the top with apples. Pour water over the apples. Stick cinnamon sticks in with them. Cover. Microwave on **HIGH** 10 minutes. Check to see if apples are fairly soft. If not, stir and continue to microwave on **HIGH** up to 6 minutes longer.

Remove from the oven but let stand with the cover on until cool. Remove cinnamon sticks. Push the apples through a strainer or mash them with a potato masher or spoon. Take a taste to see if sugar is needed. I never add sugar, but you might like it a bit sweeter.

Keep it in the refrigerator and eat it within a week. If you want to store it longer, add 2 teaspoons of lemon juice, pack it into plastic freezer bags and put it in the freezer. Makes about 4 cups.

Strawberry Pretzel Dessert

Will your friends guess the mystery ingredient in the crust of this rich dessert?

1½ cups margarine
3 cups stick pretzels, crushed
12 oz. cream cheese
¼ cup sugar
9 oz. whipped dessert topping
2 cups pineapple juice
1 pkg. (6 oz.) strawberry gelatin
2 pkg. (10 oz. each) frozen strawberries

　Place margarine in a 9 by 13-inch glass pan and cut into 5 pieces. Microwave on **MEDIUM** (50%) about 1 minute to melt. Stir in crushed pretzels. Microwave on **HIGH** 3 minutes. Cool. Unwrap cream cheese and place it in a small bowl. Microwave on **MEDIUM** (50%) about 1 to 2 minutes to barely soften. Blend in the sugar. Spread the cheese over the cooled pretzel crust. Spread dessert topping over the cream cheese. Refrigerate.

Measure pineapple juice into a 4-cup glass measuring cup. Microwave on **HIGH** about 4 to 5 minutes until boiling. Stir in gelatin and continue to stir until dissolved. Then add the frozen berries, stirring to make them separate. Refrigerate until partially set. Spread this mixture over the mixture in the pan. Refrigerate several hours or overnight. Garnish with extra topping and a few berries. Makes 12 rich servings.

Pear Crisp

This is like apple crisp, only with pears, and it's just as good.

4 medium ripe pears, peeled and sliced
5 tbs. butter or margarine
¾ cup brown sugar, packed
½ cup flour
½ cup rolled oats
¾ tsp. cinnamon
¾ tsp. nutmeg
¼ tsp. ginger

Place the pear slices in a 9-inch glass cake pan. Put the butter into a small bowl, and cut it into pieces. Microwave on **MEDIUM** (50%) 30 to 45 seconds until soft but not melted. Add all of the other ingredients and mix well. Sprinkle the mixture over the pears. Do not cover the dish. Microwave on **HIGH** 12 minutes until pears are tender. Poke with a toothpick to check. Serve with ice cream or whipped cream. Makes 6 to 8 servings.

The Main Course

The microwave oven is very good for cooking chicken and turkey. You can cook it plain to use in other recipes. You can use vegetables or sauces to make it fancy. Poultry cooks in about 7 minutes per pound.

Fish is wonderful in the microwave because it cooks quickly without smelling up the entire house. The secret to cooking fish is to cook it quickly, just until it firms and begins to flake. The general rule is 4 minutes per pound.

Warm sandwiches are included in this chapter. The key is to wrap the bread you choose in paper towels or a napkin so that the excess moisture is absorbed by the paper. This keeps the sandwich from getting soggy. But be careful, because overcooking makes bread tough and hard.

Oven Baked Fish 42	Cheese Sandwich. 48
Saucy Chicken. 43	Hot Dogs and Buns 49
Turkey Parmesan. 44	Sloppy Joes 50
Turkey Loaf 45	Tunaburgers 51
Pizza Fondue 46	Tuna Melt 52
Easy Spaghetti 47	

Oven Baked Fish

A fish fillet will cook evenly if you fold the pointed ends under and make a rectangle shape. The cornflake crumbs give a nice brown color.

1 lb. fish fillets
1 egg, slightly beaten
½ tsp. salt
dash pepper
½ cup cornflake crumbs
½ lemon
tartar sauce, if you like it

    Wash the fillets and pat them dry with a paper towel. In a wide flat dish, like a pie pan, beat the egg with salt and pepper. Place the cornflake crumbs in a second dish. Dip the fillets in egg, and then in crumbs. Put them side by side in an 8 by 12-inch glass baking pan. Tuck the pointed ends of the fish under. Cover with a paper towel or waxed paper. Microwave on **HIGH** 4 to 5 minutes until the fish is firm and flakes easily. Squeeze a few drops of lemon over each piece. Serve with tartar sauce. Makes 4 servings.

Saucy Chicken

There is enough sauce for pasta or rice, so cook some on the stove while this cooks in the microwave.

2½ to 3 lb. frying chicken, cut in pieces
1 can (10¾ oz.) cream of mushroom soup, no water added
1 can (4 oz.) mushrooms, drained
  or 10 fresh mushrooms, washed and sliced
1 tsp. salt
paprika

Remove the skin from the chicken if you don't like it. Arrange the chicken pieces in an 8 by 12-inch glass baking pan with the meaty side up and the thickest pieces on the outside. Mix soup, mushrooms and salt. Spoon the soup over the chicken. Sprinkle with paprika. Cover with waxed paper. Microwave on **HIGH** 25 to 28 minutes, rotating the dish every few minutes, until the chicken is done. Remove the chicken and spoon the sauce into a bowl to pass around. Makes 4 or 5 servings.

THE MAIN COURSE

Turkey Parmesan

My daughter asked for this so often I'm glad she finally learned to make it.

4 uncooked turkey breast slices (or use chicken)
3 tbs. margarine
½ cup cornflake crumbs
¼ cup grated Parmesan cheese

1 tsp. garlic powder
4 slices mozzarella cheese
1 can (8 oz.) marinara sauce
½ tsp. oregano

Pound the turkey with the flat side of a meat mallet or a heavy glass until it is ¼-inch thick. Cut margarine into 3 pieces and place it in an 8 by 12-inch glass pan. Microwave on **HIGH** 45 to 60 seconds to melt. Mix crumbs, cheese and garlic powder in a low flat pan.

Dip turkey slices in butter and then crumbs, coating both sides. Return to the buttered dish. Place cheese on turkey. Spread marinara sauce over the cheese. Sprinkle with oregano. Cover with waxed paper to prevent spattering tomato sauce all over the oven. Microwave on **HIGH** 6 to 7 minutes until turkey is tender. Sprinkle with more Parmesan cheese if desired. Let stand 5 minutes. Makes 4 servings.

Turkey Loaf

A bacon grill or rack especially designed for the microwave is useful for this.

1¼ lb. ground turkey
1 egg, beaten
1 can (8 oz.) tomato sauce
1 small onion, chopped fine
¼ cup chopped parsley
3 slices whole wheat bread, crumbled
1 tsp. Spice Islands Spaghetti Seasoning
2 carrots, shredded

In a large bowl, mix everything together. (This is easiest to do with clean hands.) On a microwave bacon grill that allows the fat to drip away, or in a glass pie pan, form the meat into a ring shape. Microwave on **MEDIUM** (50%) about 20 minutes. Remove to a heat-proof surface, cover with foil, and let stand 5 minutes before you cut it. Serve with chile salsa or catsup if you like it. Makes 5 to 6 servings.

Pizza Fondue

Kids of all ages love fondue. Just add a salad and you have a whole meal.

½ lb. ground beef
½ cup chopped onion
2 cans (10½ oz. each) pizza sauce
1 tbs. cornstarch
½ tsp. basil
2 tsp. oregano

¼ tsp. garlic powder
2 cups (8 oz.) grated cheddar cheese
1 cup (4 oz.) grated mozzarella cheese
1 loaf French bread, including crust, cut into cubes

Crumble beef into a 2-quart casserole and push it into a ring shape. Add onion. Microwave on **HIGH** 4 to 5 minutes, stirring after 3, until beef is no longer pink. Drain off fat. Pour pizza sauce into a 4-cup glass measuring cup or medium bowl. Add the cornstarch, basil, oregano and garlic powder. Microwave on **HIGH** 4 minutes. Add to meat. Mix cheeses. Add 1 cup to meat. Microwave on **HIGH** 1 minute. Stir. Repeat twice. Stir well.

Serve with bread cubes and fondue forks or put a pile of cubes on your plate and spoon meat sauce over. Reheat sauce on **HIGH** about 1 minute when it begins to get cool. Makes 4 to 6 servings.

Easy Spaghetti

Teamwork is called for. Adults cook the pasta. Kids make the sauce.

1 lb. ground beef or turkey sausage
1 can (15 oz.) tomato sauce
1 pkg. (1½ oz.) spaghetti sauce seasoning mix
1 cup vegetable or tomato juice
1 can (4 oz.) mushroom pieces with juice
1 can (4½ oz.) chopped ripe olives
½ cup instant chopped onion
1 pkg. (16 oz.) spaghetti, cooked
grated Parmesan cheese

Put meat in a heavy plastic colander placed over a glass pie plate, or in a casserole. Push away from center into a ring shape. Microwave on **HIGH** 6 minutes, stirring after 3. Drain. Place in a 2-quart casserole with a cover. Stir in sauce, seasoning, juice, mushrooms, olives and onions. Cover. Microwave on **HIGH** 5 minutes, stirring twice. Let stand 10 minutes. Serve over spaghetti. Sprinkle with Parmesan cheese. Makes 6 servings.

Cheese Sandwich

This sandwich is good any time of the day.

2 slices whole wheat bread
mustard, if you like it
1 slice of your favorite cheese

Toast the bread in a toaster. Place one slice on a napkin or paper plate. Spread with mustard. Top with cheese. Microwave on **HIGH** 20 to 40 seconds until the cheese starts to melt. Remove from the oven. Top with the second slice of toast and immediately turn over on the napkin. This will allow moisture on the first piece to evaporate. Cut in half. Makes 1 serving.

A Good Idea

Add a slice of ham or other meat to the toast before you put on the cheese. Add 10 to 20 seconds to the heating time.

Hot Dogs and Buns

This is the best method for cooking hot dogs, because the paper absorbs the fat from the wieners. You'll think you are at the ball park.

1 to 6 buns
1 to 6 wieners

If buns are frozen, defrost them first. Wrap in a paper towel or a kitchen towel and microwave on **HIGH** 10 seconds for each. Remove from oven. Wrap the same number of wieners tightly in a paper towel. Microwave on **HIGH**:

1 wiener	10 seconds
2 wieners	30 seconds
4 wieners	45 seconds
6 wieners	45 seconds

Place wrapped buns in the oven with the wieners and microwave on **HIGH** 30 seconds for 1 to 6 wieners. Do not overcook as the wieners will split and the buns will toughen.

THE MAIN COURSE

Sloppy Joes

This hamburger filling has been a favorite of the kids in my cooking classes.

1 lb. ground beef
1 onion, chopped
⅓ cup catsup
2 tsp. vinegar
6 hamburger buns, split

2 tsp. lemon juice
1 tbs. Worcestershire sauce
½ tsp. prepared mustard
2 tsp. brown sugar

Crumble beef into a heavy plastic colander placed in a glass pie plate or in a 2-quart casserole. Shape in a ring, pushing meat from the middle. Add chopped onions. Microwave on **HIGH** 6 to 7 minutes, stirring once, until meat is no longer pink. Drain fat and juices. Add the remaining ingredients except the buns. Stir well. Cover. Microwave on **HIGH** 6 to 7 minutes, stirring twice, until hot. Spoon over buns. Makes 6 servings.

A Good Idea
Serve leftover Sloppy Joe filling on hot baked potatoes. Yum!

Tunaburgers

When you need a change from hamburgers, get out the tuna.

4 hamburger buns
¼ cup mayonnaise, divided
2 tbs. catsup
sweet pickle slices
4 slices process cheese

1 can (6½ oz.) tuna, drained
1 tbs. chopped onion
¼ cup finely chopped celery
1 tsp. lemon juice
dash garlic powder

Slice buns and open. Mix 2 tbs. mayonnaise with catsup. Spread on the bottom of each bun. Cover with pickle slices and cheese. Mix together tuna, onion, celery, lemon juice, garlic powder and remaining mayonnaise. Spread on the cheese. Place buns on a paper towel in the oven. Cover with another paper towel. Microwave on **HIGH** 1½ minutes until hot. Makes 4 servings.

Tuna Melt

Everything you need to make this is probably on the shelf right now. Go to it!

2 pita breads, English muffins or hamburger buns
1 can (6½ oz.) tuna, drained
3 tbs. mayonnaise
1 stalk celery, chopped fine, if you like it
1 tsp. pickle relish
4 slices tomato
4 slices cheese, your favorite kind

    Cut the bread in half. Toast in a toaster. In a small bowl, mix the tuna, mayonnaise, celery and pickle relish. Divide among the breads, spreading to the edges of each. Put a tomato slice on each. Top with cheese. Cover a plate with a paper towel and place tuna buns in a circle on it. Microwave on **HIGH** 1½ to 3 minutes just until cheese melts. Makes 2 to 4 servings.

Casseroles

Casserole is the name for a covered baking dish in which food can be cooked and served. It is also the name of the food cooked in such a dish. Usually, a casserole is made from any combination of grain (like rice) or pasta, meat, fish or cheese, and vegetables. There can be many ingredients in a casserole, but it is usually very easy to make.

If you are a beginner, there are ways to make it even easier. You can use frozen vegetables that are already chopped. You can use leftover meat. You can buy cheese that is already shredded.

Often, you can put a casserole together ahead of time and put it in the refrigerator. If you refrigerate a casserole, add 1 to 3 minutes to the final cooking time. When pasta or rice is called for, it is usually easier to cook it on the top of the stove. An older person should do this if you are a beginner.

Casseroles are usually very filling. All you need to add is a green salad or a fruit salad, a roll and dessert to make a meal. Great for busy families!

Hamburger Stroganoff 55
Easy Lasagna 56
Lasagna Whirls 58
Chopstick Tuna . . . 59
Tuna Noodle Casserole . 60
Beef Taco Casserole . . . 61
Chicken Enchilladas 62
Sunday Night Supper . . 63
Tuna Macaroni Casserole . 64
Chicken Casserole . . . 65
Macaroni and Cheese . . 66

Hamburger Stroganoff

Have an adult cook noodles or rice while you prepare the topping.

1 lb. ground beef
1 small onion, chopped, or ½ cup frozen chopped onion
1 can (10¾ oz.) cream of mushroom soup, no water added
1 can (4 oz.) mushrooms with juice or 10 fresh mushrooms, washed and sliced
1 pkg. (4 grams) beef broth and seasoning mix
1 cup (½ pint) sour cream, sour half-and-half, or plain yogurt

Crumble the beef and onion in 1½ quart casserole, pushing it away from the center to form a ring. Microwave on **HIGH** 6 minutes, stirring after 3 minutes, until meat is no longer pink. Drain off as much fat as possible. Add remaining ingredients, stirring well. Cover. Microwave on **HIGH** 7 to 8 minutes until heated through. Do not allow to boil or sour cream will curdle. Serve over noodles or rice. Makes 4 to 5 servings.

Easy Lasagna

The no-cook method for the noodles makes this easy for beginners.

1 jar (32 oz.) spaghetti sauce with meat
½ cup water
1 egg, beaten
2 cups ricotta or cottage cheese
½ tsp. pepper
8 uncooked lasagna noodles
2 pkg. (6 oz. each) sliced mozzarella cheese
½ cup grated Parmesan cheese

In a large bowl, mix spaghetti sauce with water. In a medium bowl, beat the egg with a fork. Stir in ricotta or cottage cheese and pepper. Spread ⅓ cup tomato sauce in the bottom of an 8 by 12-inch glass pan. Arrange 4 noodles in a single layer over the sauce. Top with half the ricotta cheese mixture, and then a package of mozarrella cheese slices. Spread with 1 cup of spaghetti sauce. Then do it again -- tomato sauce, noodles, ricotta, mozzarella, spaghetti sauce.

Cover tightly with microwave-safe plastic wrap. Turn back one corner to vent steam. Microwave on **HIGH** 8 minutes and on **MEDIUM** (50%) for 30 to 32 minutes until noodles are tender. Rotate pan twice during cooking. Uncover, being careful to peel back plastic without burning face or hands. Top with Parmesan cheese. Let stand 15 minutes to melt cheese and make cutting easy. Makes 6 servings.

Lasagne Whirls

When there are just a few lasagne noodles left in the box, think of this.

4 lasagne noodles
1 cup cottage cheese
1 cup (4 oz.) shredded mozzarella cheese
1 jar (14 oz.) meat-flavored spaghetti sauce
2 tbs. grated Parmesan cheese

Cook noodles using the directions on the noodle package. Drain them, and pat them dry with paper towels. Place them on a flat surface, like a cutting board. Mix the cottage cheese with the mozzarella. Spread it on the noodles, dividing it evenly. Roll up each noodle and place it with the seam side down in a microwave-safe dish or square glass cake pan. Pour the sauce over the noodles. Cover with waxed paper to prevent tomato spatters. Microwave on **HIGH** 5 to 6 minutes until hot. Sprinkle with cheese. Microwave on **HIGH** 1 minute, uncovered, until cheese begins to melt. Makes 2 to 4 servings.

Chopstick Tuna

This recipe was probably cooked by your mother, your grandmother, and maybe your great-grandmother! The microwave makes it faster.

1 can (10¾ oz.) cream of mushroom soup, no water added
1 cup (½ of a 3 oz. can) chow mein noodles
1 can (6½, 7 or 9½ oz.) tuna, drained
1 cup sliced celery
¼ cup chopped onion
½ cup chopped salted cashews or peanuts
dash pepper
1½ tsp. soy sauce

In a 2-quart casserole, mix all the ingredients. Cover the casserole with waxed paper. Microwave on **HIGH** 6 minutes. Stir. Microwave on **MEDIUM** (50%) 6 minutes. Let stand 5 minutes before serving. Add a few more noodles for garnish if you want to. Makes 4 to 5 servings.

A Good Idea

Use 2 cups cubed leftover turkey or chicken instead of tuna.

Tuna Noodle Casserole

Have an older person help you cook the noodles for this yummy dish.

6 oz. (about 3½ cups) noodles
2 cups potato chips, crushed
1 can (6½ or 7 oz.) chunk style tuna
1 can (10¾ oz.) cream of mushroom
  or cream of chicken soup, no water added

    Follow the package directions to cook the noodles. Drain them. Place half of the crushed potato chips in a 1½-quart casserole. Open the tuna can, but do not remove the lid. Push it down on the tuna, and turn the can over at the sink to drain off the liquid. Push hard. Add the tuna to the chips. Use a fork to break the tuna into small pieces. Add soup and noodles. Stir well. Microwave on **HIGH** 6 to 7 minutes, uncovered, stirring after 4 minutes. When the casserole is hot, sprinkle the other half of the potato chips over the top. Microwave on **HIGH** 1 to 2 minutes longer. Makes 4 servings.

CASSEROLES

Beef Taco Casserole

Make it ahead of time and refrigerate — it tastes even better.

1 lb. ground beef
2 cans (8 oz. each) tomato sauce or 1 can (15 oz.) enchillada sauce
1/2 cup chopped onion
1 tbs. chili powder (more if you like it spicy hot)
1/2 tsp. salt
1/4 tsp. pepper
6 medium (6 inch) corn tortillas, torn into pieces about 2 x 2 inches
1 1/2 cups (6 oz.) grated cheddar cheese, divided
1 can (2 1/2 oz.) sliced ripe olives

Crumble the beef into a heavy plastic colander over a glass pie plate. Push it toward the edges, making it look like a doughnut. Microwave on **HIGH** 3 minutes. Stir to break the meat into smaller pieces. Microwave on **HIGH** 3 minutes until meat loses its red color. Drain. In a 4-cup glass measuring cup or bowl, mix the sauce, onion, chili powder, salt and pepper. Cover with plastic wrap, leaving a small area uncovered. Microwave on **HIGH** 5 minutes. Stir. In a 2 1/2- or 3-quart casserole with cover, mix beef, sauce, tortillas, 1 cup cheese and olives. Stir well. Cover. Microwave on **HIGH** 4 minutes. Stir. Microwave on **HIGH** 3 to 4 minutes until very hot and cheese is melted. Remove cover. Add 1/2 cup cheese. Microwave on **HIGH** 30 seconds. Makes 4 to 6 servings.

Chicken Enchilladas

This recipe is fun to make, and everyone will love it.

1 can (10¾ oz.) cream of mushroom soup
½ cup water
1 cup diced cooked chicken or 1 can (5 oz.) boned chicken
3 green onions, sliced

1 tbs. diced green chiles (if you like them)
1 cup shredded mozzarella cheese
4 flour tortillas
½ cup shredded cheddar cheese
4 tbs. sour cream
4 tbs. chili salsa

In a small bowl, stir together soup and water. In another bowl, mix chicken, green onions, chiles and mozzarella cheese. Wrap flour tortillas in a paper towel. Microwave on **HIGH** 20 to 30 seconds to soften. Spread them on a board. Divide the chicken on the tortillas. Spread half the soup mixture in an 8 by 8-inch square glass pan. Roll up tortillas and place them in the pan with the seam side down. Pour the remaining soup on top. Microwave on **HIGH** 6 minutes. Sprinkle with cheddar cheese and microwave on **HIGH** 2 to 3 minutes until cheese is melted. Let stand about 5 minutes before serving. Top each with a tablespoon of sour cream and a tablespoon of salsa. Makes 2 to 4 servings.

Sunday Night Supper

*Slice canned brown bread in 8 pieces, wrap in a paper towel, and microwave on **HIGH** about 1 minute. Enjoy it with your beans and franks.*

1 can (28 oz.) baked beans
3 tbs. brown sugar
1/4 cup catsup
1/2 tsp. Worcestershire sauce
2 tbs. dried onion flakes
1 tbs. light molasses
8 frankfurters, cut up, or 1 lb. cocktail weiners

Open the beans and throw away the chunks of fat. Pour the beans into a 1½ quart casserole. Add everything else. Cover. Microwave on **HIGH** 7 to 8 minutes, stirring twice. Makes 4 servings.

Tuna Macaroni Casserole

Start with a package of macaroni and cheese for a quick supper.

1 pkg. (6¼ or 7¼) Macaroni and Cheddar
4 tbs. butter or margarine
¼ cup milk
1 can (6½ or 7 oz.) tuna, drained
1 can (8 oz.) peas, drained, or 1 cup frozen peas, uncooked

Have an older person help you cook the macaroni. Cook it in 2 quarts of rapidly boiling water on top the the stove for 8 minutes. Drain it. Put it in a 2-quart casserole. Mix in the butter, milk and cheese from the package. Drain the tuna. (Open the can, leave on the lid, push down hard on it and turn it over in the sink to drain.) Add tuna and peas and stir gently with a fork. Microwave on **HIGH** 5 minutes until bubbly. Makes 3 to 4 servings.

A Good Idea

Instead of tuna, you can add 1 cup of chopped leftover cooked meat or chicken.

Chicken Casserole

This is the easiest main dish, because all you need to do is open cans. Your mom may remember making something like this when she was in school.

2 cans (6½ or 7 oz. each) chicken meat
½ cup milk
1 can (8½ oz.) peas or 1 cup frozen peas, uncooked
1 can (13½ oz.) condensed cream of chicken soup, no water added
2 cups crushed potato chips

Mix everything except ½ cup crushed chips in a 2-quart casserole. Microwave on **HIGH** 4 minutes, uncovered. Stir. Cover with remaining chips. Microwave on **HIGH** 3 to 4 minutes longer until heated through. Makes 4 servings.

A Good Idea
Use canned tuna and cream of mushroom soup.

Macaroni and Cheese

This is everyone's favorite. Get an older person to help you cook the noodles.

1½ quarts (6 cups) boiling water
2 cups (8 oz.) elbow macaroni
½ tsp. salt
3 tbs. margarine
3 tbs. flour
1 tsp. salt
½ tsp. pepper
½ tsp. dried chives, if you like them
1½ cups milk
2 cups (8 oz.) grated cheese (sharp cheddar or any favorite)
1½ tbs. corn flakes crumbs or seasoned bread crumbs

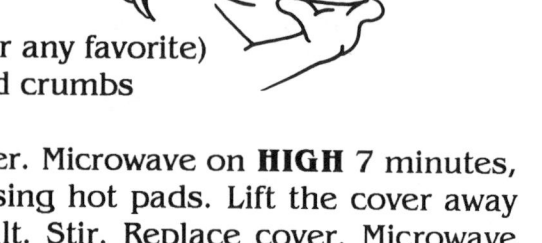

Measure water into a 3-quart casserole. Cover. Microwave on **HIGH** 7 minutes, until water boils. Remove from microwave, using hot pads. Lift the cover away from your face. Add macaroni and ½ tsp. salt. Stir. Replace cover. Microwave on **HIGH** 7 minutes. Let stand 3 to 4 minutes to finish cooking.

Carefully remove the lid and drain the macaroni through a strainer. Stir to get macaroni as dry as possible.

Place margarine in a 1-quart casserole. Cut into 3 pieces. Microwave on HIGH 45 to 50 seconds. Stir in flour until smooth. Microwave on **HIGH** 30 to 45 seconds until bubbly. Add salt, pepper, chives and milk. Microwave on **HIGH** 4 to 5 minutes, stirring after each minute, until thick and just beginning to rise in the dish. Add cheese and stir until melted. Place well-drained macaroni in the 3-quart casserole. Add cheese sauce. Stir to mix evenly. Microwave on **HIGH** 3 minutes, uncovered. Stir again. Top with crumbs. Microwave on **HIGH**, uncovered, about 2 minutes until heated through. Makes 6 to 8 servings.

A Good Idea

Add 2 cups of cubed ham, turkey or frankfurters. You may also use processed cheese such as Velveeta.

Veggies

The microwave cooks vegetables perfectly. You don't work as hard, and the vegetables taste better. The color stays brighter, so they are prettier, and they keep more vitamins and minerals. When you cook your own vegetables, you will really like them. You'll find old favorites here, and some new ideas.

Acorn Squash 69	Yam and Apple Casserole . . 78
Orange Glazed Carrots . . . 70	Fresh Yams 79
Corn on the Cob 71	Baked Potatoes 80
Corn Pudding 72	'Tater Toppings: 'Taters with Cheese Sauce 81
Green Bean Bake 73	
Veggie Bobs 74	'Tater Toppings: 'Tater Tacos 82
Tomato Zucchini Dish . . . 76	'Tater Toppings: 'Tuna Topper 83
Orange Scalloped Sweet Potatoes 77	'Tater Toppings: Morris's Favorite 84

Acorn Squash

If you cook squash of any kind before you cut it open, it makes the job a cinch.

2 medium acorn squash
4 tbs. brown sugar
4 tsp. butter or margarine

Wash squash. Stick a heavy kitchen fork into it several times. Place on a paper plate or a paper towel-lined plate. Microwave on **HIGH** 6 minutes. Turn over. Microwave on **HIGH** 5 or 6 minutes until soft. Cut squash in half: be careful, because it is very hot. Carefully remove seeds and stringy pulp. (You may wish to save the seeds to use in the **Toasted Pumpkin Seeds** recipe on page 115.)

With squash cut side up on a plate, add 1 tbs. brown sugar and 1 tbs. butter to the middle of each half. Microwave on **HIGH** 2 minutes until butter and sugar begin to carmelize. Makes 4 servings.

Orange Glazed Carrots

The orange sauce makes these special.

1 lb. carrots, peeled and sliced
1/4 tsp. salt
dash nutmeg
3 tbs. orange juice
2 tsp. butter or margarine

Combine all ingredients in a 1-quart casserole. Cover. Microwave on **HIGH** 6 to 7 minutes, stirring after 3 minutes and again after 6 minutes. Carrots should be barely soft. Let stand 5 minutes. Makes 4 to 6 servings.

A Good Idea

If you are a beginner you could start with 1 lb. frozen cut carrots. Defrost according to directions on package, and then follow this recipe. You won't have to peel and slice.

Corn on the Cob

The all-time favorite is easy to handle when cooked with this method.

4 medium ears of corn
butter or margarine
salt and pepper to taste

Cut 4 large squares of waxed paper. Remove the husks from the corn and pull off the silk. Run under cold water but do not dry. Immediately roll the corn in the paper, leaving the ends open. Place in the microwave in a single layer. Microwave on **HIGH** 6 to 8 minutes, depending on size. Rearrange after 4 minutes. Wait 1 minute before slipping the corn out of the paper. Serve with butter, salt and pepper. Makes 4 servings.

Corn Pudding

This is a good recipe for first-time cooks. You can beat the egg, crush the crackers, and stir everything right in the same dish.

1 egg
¾ cup crushed saltine crackers (about 14 squares)
1 can (17 oz.) cream style corn
salt and pepper to taste
paprika

Break the egg into a 1-quart casserole. Beat well with a fork. Crush crackers directly over the egg, or place in a plastic bag and squeeze or pound to break up. Add corn, salt and pepper and stir well. Microwave on **MEDIUM** (50%) 8 minutes, stirring every 2 minutes. Sprinkle with paprika. Microwave on **MEDIUM** 2 minutes until nearly set. Let it stand a few minutes before serving. Makes 4 servings.

Green Bean Bake

Double this recipe and make a dish for company.

1 pkg. (9 oz.) frozen French style green beans
½ can (2.8 oz.) French fried onion rings
½ can (10¾ oz.) cream of mushroom soup, no water added
¼ cup seasoned bread crumbs, or croutons, or corn flake crumbs

Place beans in a 1-quart casserole. Cover. Microwave on **HIGH** 6 to 8 minutes, stirring twice to break up. Let stand 3 minutes. Stir in onion rings and soup. Top with remaining onion rings and crumbs. Do not cover. Microwave on **HIGH** 3 to 4 minutes until hot. Let stand 3 minutes before serving. Makes 3 to 4 servings.

A Good Idea

Instead of green beans, use frozen or fresh broccoli that has been cut into small pieces.

Veggie Bobs

Colorful kabobs are such fun to eat, you forget they are good for you too. Make certain all vegetables are cut to about the same size for even cooking.

1 medium zucchini, cut into 8 chunks
8 cherry tomatoes
8 pieces of pepper (red, green or yellow)
8 onion quarters
¾ cup oil and vinegar or Italian salad dressing
¼ cup water
¼ cup soy sauce

Wash the vegetables and cut them up. Thread them on 4 wooden skewers. Put 2 pieces of each kind of vegetable on each skewer. In a large sealable plastic bag or plastic container with a tight cover, mix the salad dressing, water and soy sauce. Place the skewers with vegetables in the bag and seal tightly. Marinate several hours, turning several times.

To cook, remove vegetable skewers from bag and place on a microwave meat rack or an 8 by 12-inch glass pan. Cover with waxed paper to prevent spatters.

Microwave on **HIGH** 4 minutes. Turn over and rotate positions so that the 2 outside skewers are now in the middle. Microwave on **HIGH** 3 to 4 minutes until the vegetables are nearly tender. Let stand 5 minutes before serving. If you like it, sprinkle with a lemon herb seasoning. Makes 4 servings.

VEGGIES

Tomato Zucchini Dish

Check the refrigerator before making this. Maybe there are other vegetables you would like to add.

2 medium zucchini, cut into slices or small chunks
1 medium tomato, chopped
4 green onions, sliced, or ¼ yellow onion, sliced
¼ cup chopped pepper (green, red or yellow)
¼ tsp. garlic salt
1 tsp. tarragon
¼ cup grated Parmesan cheese

Mix zucchini, tomato, onions and pepper in a 2-quart casserole with a lid. Sprinkle with garlic salt and tarragon. Cover. Microwave on **HIGH** 6 to 7 minutes. Carefully drain. Uncover. Stir. Sprinkle with cheese. Microwave on **HIGH** 2 minutes, without cover, until vegetables are tender. Let stand 5 minutes before serving. Makes 4 servings.

Orange Scalloped Sweet Potatoes

You've probably eaten scalloped potatoes, but have you tried scalloped sweet potatoes?

½ cup unsweetened applesauce
½ cup brown sugar
¼ cup orange juice
½ tsp. ground nutmeg
1 tbs. butter or margarine
3 medium sweet potatoes, about 1½ lbs.

In a 2-cup glass measuring cup, mix applesauce, brown sugar, orange juice and nutmeg. Add butter. Microwave on **HIGH** 3 minutes, stirring every minute. Set aside. You might need an adult to help you peel the potatoes and cut them into thin slices. Put a layer of potatoes into a 1½-quart casserole with a cover. Spoon 2 tablespoons of orange sauce over the potato slices. Continue to layer, ending with sauce. Cover. Microwave on **HIGH** 12 minutes. Remove from oven. With a small ladle, spoon sauce from the bottom of the dish over the potatoes. Microwave on **HIGH** 3 to 4 minutes longer. Let stand, covered, 10 minutes before serving. Makes 6 servings.

Yam and Apple Casserole

Good anytime, but really wonderful for Thanksgiving. You can help put it together the day before and refrigerate it (add 1 minute to the final cooking time).

1 can (16 oz.) cut yams
2 medium apples, cored and peeled
2 tbs. brown sugar
1 tbs. butter or margarine
2 tbs. maple syrup
1 tbs. apple or orange juice
½ tsp. cinnamon
¼ tsp. ground ginger

Drain yams. Place them in a 1-quart casserole with a lid. Cut apples in chunks and add them. In a small bowl or 1-cup glass measuring cup, place the remaining ingredients. Stir. Microwave on **HIGH** 1½ to 2 minutes until bubbling, but watch so that it doesn't boil over. Pour over yams and apples. Cover. Microwave on **HIGH** 4 to 5 minutes until heated. Makes 4 servings.

A Good Idea

To double the recipe, use a large can of yams and 3 to 4 apples in a 2-quart casserole. Do not double the sauce ingredients (all the ingredients starting with brown sugar). Microwave on **HIGH** 8 minutes, until well heated. Makes 8 servings.

Fresh Yams

If you wish to use fresh yams in the **Yam and Apple Casserole,** wash 2 pounds of yams. Poke each with a heavy kitchen fork in several places. Arrange the yams in a circle on a double piece of paper towel or heavy duty paper plate. Microwave on **HIGH** 15 minutes until slightly soft. Remove from oven and wrap in a fabric towel. Allow to stand 10 minutes. When cool enough to handle, peel and cut into 1/4-inch slices.

When preparing apples, cut slices a similar size so so everything will cook evenly. Stir together in a 2-quart casserole. This time, double the sauce ingredients. Cover and microwave on **HIGH** 8 minutes until hot. Makes 8 to 10 servings.

Baked Potatoes

Choose firm medium potatoes of similar shape and size (6 to 7 ounces each, about the size of a woman's fist). Rinse and pat dry. Poke with a heavy kitchen fork to allow steam to escape. If you don't, they might explode and make a big mess. Place on a heavy paper plate or a double layer of paper towels. Arrange in a circle, not touching. Microwave on **HIGH** according to the chart. After half the cooking time, turn the potatoes over, and rearrange them if your oven does not have a turntable. When cooking time is over, they should barely make a dent when pushed. Remove the potatoes from oven and wrap in a cloth towel for 10 minutes or longer. The cooking will finish, the temperature will equalize, and the potatoes will become soft. The towel helps dry and crisp the skin. To serve, cut an X on top and push the ends together.

Microwave on High for Baking Potatoes and Sweet Potatoes

1 potato	4 to 6 minutes
2 potatoes	7 to 8 minutes
3 potatoes	11 to 13 minutes
4 potatoes	14 to 16 minutes
6 potatoes	16 to 18 minutes

'Tater Toppings: 'Taters with Cheese Sauce

Baked potatoes can be the base for a filling lunch or an easy supper. Anything can be added. Try these for starters.

2 tbs. magarine
1/4 cup flour
1 1/4 cups milk
1 1/2 cups (6 oz.) grated
  sharp cheddar cheese

1/2 tsp. dry mustard
salt and pepper
4 to 6 baked potatoes

Place margarine in a 4-cup glass measuring cup. Microwave on **HIGH** 45 to 60 seconds until bubbly. With a whisk or fork, stir in flour until completely blended. Add milk slowly, stirring until smooth. Microwave on **HIGH** 1 1/2 to 2 minutes until sauce thickens. Stir well. Add cheese, stirring to help it melt. Microwave on **MEDIUM** (50%) 1 minute if necessary to melt cheese. Add dry mustard, salt and pepper. Tops 4 to 6 potatoes.

'Tater Toppings: 'Tater Tacos

½ lb. ground beef or turkey
¼ cup chopped onion
½ pkg. (¼ oz.) taco seasoning
water
grated Monterey Jack or cheddar cheese
1 tomato, chopped fine
sour cream, if you like it
guacamole
4 baked potatoes

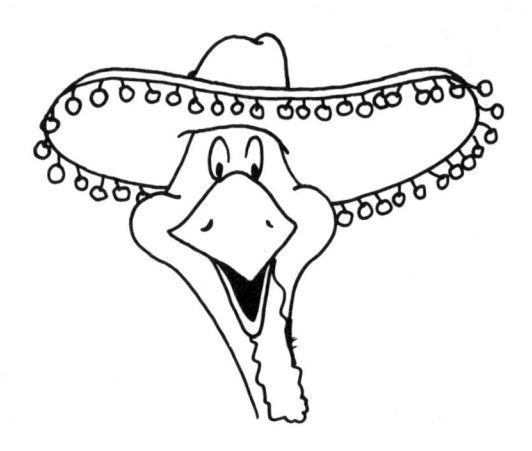

Crumble beef into a heavy plastic colander set over a glass pie plate, or put beef into a glass cake dish. Add onion. Microwave on **HIGH** 3 minutes, stirring about 1½ minutes. Drain. Add taco seasoning and half of the water the package asks for. Microwave on **HIGH** 2½ to 3 minutes. Divide over 4 baked potatoes. Top with cheese, sour cream, guacamole and chopped tomatoes. Makes 4 servings.

'Tater Toppings: Tuna 'Taters

1 can (6½ oz.) tuna
½ cup chopped onion
¼ cup chopped green pepper
1 tbs. water
1 cup frozen peas or corn

1 cup (4 oz.) shredded cheddar cheese
½ cup margarine
2 tbs. milk
1 tsp. lemon juice
4 baked potatoes

Open tuna and drain well by pushing the lid hard against the tuna as you turn the can over at the sink. In a 4-cup glass measuring cup, combine the onion, green pepper and water. Cover with plastic wrap, leaving one area uncovered to vent. Microwave on **HIGH** 2 to 2½ minutes until vegetables are tender. Carefully remove plastic away from your face. Add peas or corn. Microwave on **HIGH** 1 minute. Stir in remaining ingredients except potatoes.

Cut potatoes in half and place them on a platter. Divide the filling over the potatoes. Cover with waxed paper. Microwave on **MEDIUM HIGH** (70%) 5 to 7 minutes until the cheese is melted and topping is hot. Makes 4 servings.

'Tater Toppings: Morris's Favorite

This is my favorite baked potato topping. I hope you like it, too.

1 baked potato
½ cup broccoli, cooked
½ cup cottage cheese

2 tbs. chile salsa
1 tbs. grated Parmesan cheese
   (freshly grated is best)

Cut the potato in half and put it on a plate. Put broccoli on top of each potato. Cover with cottage cheese. Put 1 tablespoon of salsa on each half. Microwave on **HIGH** about 1 minute to slightly melt cheese. Sprinkle with Parmesan cheese. Makes 1 serving.

Other 'Tater Toppings

bacon bits
chopped onions
grated cheese
chile salsa
peas
sour cream

butter
grated or sliced carrots
zucchini
alfalfa sprouts
leftover anything: chili, soup, stew,
   vegetables, any diced meat

Desserts

I'll bet if I ask you what the best part of a meal is, your answer is sure to be dessert. Once snacks are mastered, you should try desserts. They are easy to make and can be ready much faster in a microwave. Desserts teach you to follow directions, to measure, and to mix. They teach you about after-cooking (the standing time needed after the microwave cooking time), which allows the internal temperature to equalize, the top to dry, and the cooking process to finish.

Use the cooking time to clean up the kitchen, a very good habit to get into. These recipes show you the most commonly used steps for dessert-making. After you learn them, you can make other family favorites in the microwave.

Vanilla Pudding	86	Frosty Lemon Pie.	94
PB and J Pudding	87	Cookie Crumb Crust.	95
Plum Good Bars	88	Graham Cracker Crust	96
Bread Pudding	89	Mud Pie	97
Ginger Spice Bars	90	Hot Fudge Sauce.	98
Lemon Icing	91	Caramel Sauce	99
Apple Upside-Down Cake	92	Praline Sauce	100
One-Dish Brownies	93	Custard Sauce.	101

Vanilla Pudding

Pudding from scratch is almost as easy as from a mix, but the taste is much better.

¾ cup sugar
2 tbs. cornstarch
2 cups milk

2 egg yolks
1 tsp. vanilla

In a 2-quart bowl or 8-cup glass measure, mix sugar and cornstarch. Stir in milk. Microwave on **HIGH** 5 minutes, stirring after 2 minutes and then each minute, until mixture has thickened and just begins to boil. Beat egg yolks with a fork in a small bowl. Add 3 tablespoons hot milk, 1 tablespoon at a time, to warm the yolks. Stir the warmed yolks into the hot milk. Microwave on **HIGH** 2 minutes until the mixture just begins to rise. Remove from oven. Stir in vanilla. To prevent skin from forming, press waxed paper on the top. Serve warm or cool. Makes 4 servings.

A Good Idea: Chocolate Pudding

Add 1 cup semisweet chocolate pieces with the vanilla. Stir until they dissolve.

PB and J Pudding

Is there anyone alive who doesn't like peanut butter and jelly?

1 pkg. (3¾ oz.) vanilla pudding and pie filling, *not* instant
2 cups milk
¼ cup peanut butter
4 tsp. jelly, your favorite

    Empty pudding mix into a 4-cup glass measuring cup. Add ½ cup milk. Stir until well blended. Add remaining milk. Microwave on **HIGH** 6 to 8 minutes, stirring every 3 minutes, until pudding is thick. Add peanut butter and stir in well. Spoon into 4 custard cups or serving dishes. Chill. Just before serving, add a teaspoon of jelly to each cup. Makes 4 servings.

DESSERTS

Plum Good Bars

This is a very good choice if you are a beginner, because there is no chopping.

1 can (17 oz.) plums
2 tsp. brown sugar
1 tsp. cinnamon
½ cup margarine
1¼ cups rolled oats
¾ cup flour
¼ cup brown sugar

Drain plums. Using clean hands, push the stone out of each and pull it apart. Place the plums in a small bowl. Stir in brown sugar and set aside.

Place margarine in an 8-inch square glass cake pan. Microwave on **HIGH** 45 to 60 seconds to melt. Add remaining ingredients and stir to blend. Remove ½ cup. Use fingers to press the oat mixture in the bottom of the pan. Microwave on **HIGH** 2 minutes. Spread plums on the crust. Crumble remaining oat mixture over plums. Microwave on **HIGH** 2 to 4 minutes until set. Let stand 20 minutes or more. Cut into 2 by 2-inch squares. Makes 16 bars.

Bread Pudding

Bread that is too old for sandwiches is perfect for pudding. For a unique flavor, use a variety of breads, buns and muffins. Include the crusts for more color.

4 cups torn bread cubes, about 8 slices
2 whole eggs plus 2 whites
1/3 cup sugar
2 cups milk

1/2 cup golden or seedless raisins
1 tsp. vanilla extract
1/2 tsp. ground cinnamon
2 tbs. sugar

Place bread cubes in a 2-quart casserole. In a small bowl, beat eggs with a fork until mixed. Add 1/3 cup sugar and milk. Stir until sugar is dissolved. Add raisins and extract. Pour over bread. Let sit 30 to 60 minutes. Microwave on **HIGH** 4 minutes. Meanwhile combine cinnamon and 2 tbs. sugar. Remove pudding from oven. Sprinkle sugar mix over top. Microwave on **MEDIUM** (50%) 8 to 10 minutes until just set. Remove to a flat heat-proof surface such as a wooden board to finish setting. Cool slightly or serve cold. Serve with **Custard Sauce**, page 101, if you like it. Makes 6 servings.

Ginger Spice Bars

If you cook the batter with a glass in the center and raise the pan, the batter will cook more evenly and you won't have a soggy center.

1 pkg. (14 oz.) gingerbread mix
1 cup applesauce
½ cup raisins

Lightly spray an 8-inch square glass pan with no-stick cooking spray. In a mixing bowl, stir the mix, applesauce and raisins until no dry mix remains. Spread evenly in the pan. Press a small glass, bottom side down, into the center of the pan. Place the pan in the oven on an overturned plate or large cereal bowl. Microwave on **MEDIUM** (50%) for 6 minutes, rotating pan ¼ turn every 2 minutes. Cook on **HIGH** 2 to 5 minutes, just until there are no wet spots. Top should spring back if touched lightly, but be careful: it's hot. Do not overcook. Remove to a heat-proof surface such as a wooden board to finish cooking. Frost when cool if you want to. Makes 20 to 24 bars.

Lemon Icing

1 cup powdered sugar
1 tbs. margarine, softened
2 tsp. lemon juice
1 tbs. milk

In a small deep bowl, combine all ingredients. Use a fork to stir until smooth. Use a knife or small spatula to frost bars or cake. Cut into serving pieces when firm.

Apple Upside-Down Cake

It frosts itself when you turn it over!

3 tbs. butter or margarine
½ cup brown sugar, firmly packed
1 tsp. cinnamon
1½ cups grated apple (about 1 large)

1 cup raisins
½ cup chopped walnuts, if you like them
2 cups yellow cake mix (1-layer pkg. or ½ of a 2-layer pkg.

Place butter in an 8-inch round glass pan or 9-inch Corningware skillet. Microwave on HIGH 45 to 60 seconds to melt. Add brown sugar, cinnamon, grated apples and raisins. Add nuts if using. Mix and spread smooth. Prepare cake mix according to package directions. (If using a 2-layer cake mix, use half the water called for.) Spread evenly over the apple mixture. Cover with waxed paper. Microwave on **MEDIUM** (50%) 4 to 5 minutes, rotating pan ½ turn after every minute. Microwave on **HIGH** 2 to 3 minutes until just dry.

Remove to a heat-proof surface such as a wooden board. Let stand 5 minutes before turning out over a plate or platter. Serve with whipped cream or ice cream if you like it. Makes 8 servings.

One-Dish Brownies

If you love to eat, but hate to wash dishes, this recipe is for you.

2/3 cup vegetable shortening
1 cup sugar
2 eggs, beaten
1 tsp. vanilla
1 cup flour
1/2 tsp. baking powder
1/2 tsp. salt
1/2 cup dry cocoa
1/2 cup chopped nuts

Place shortening in an 8-inch square glass baking pan. Microwave on **HIGH** about 2 minutes. Stir in sugar. Cool. Add beaten eggs and vanilla. Beat with a fork until well blended. Measure flour, baking powder, salt and cocoa into a sifter. Sift into the glass pan. Stir to blend. Smooth batter. Sprinkle nuts on top. Cover with waxed paper. Microwave on **HIGH** about 5 minutes, rotating pan every minute after the first 2. When top is almost dry, remove from oven to a heat-proof surface. Frost now with *Quick Frosting* or allow to cool. Cut when cold. Makes 16 squares.

Quick Frosting

Immediately after you take it out of the oven, sprinkle with a 6 oz. package of chocolate chips. When soft, about 10 minutes, spread evenly over the top.

Frosty Lemon Pie

There are other flavors in the world besides chocolate. Here are two of the best.

1 **Cookie Crumb Crust**, page 95, cooled (gingersnap is best)
1 qt. frozen nonfat yogurt, vanilla

1 can (6 oz.) frozen lemonade, thawed
¼ tsp. lemon extract
Raspberry Sauce

Remove cover from yogurt. Microwave on **HIGH** 15 seconds to soften. Remove lemonade from metal can. Place in a large bowl and microwave on **HIGH** 15 to 30 seconds. Combine with yogurt and extract. Spoon into pie shell. Cover with plastic wrap. Return to freezer for several hours or overnight. Just before serving, drizzle with *Raspberry Sauce*. Makes 6 to 8 servings.

Raspberry Sauce

Place 1 package frozen raspberries in a medium bowl. Microwave on **DEFROST** (10%) 5 to 10 minutes. Use a fork to separate berries, but do not heat. Crush with a fork. Add 2 tbs. sugar if needed. Drizzle over cut pie wedges before you serve them.

Cookie Crumb Crust

Be creative. Use whatever cookies are your favorite.

1 1/3 cups cookie crumbs (gingersnaps, Oreos, chocolate wafers, oatmeal, chocolate chip)
6 tbs. butter or margarine

  Be sure cookies are finely crushed. They should look like ground coffee. Since they have sugar in them, you do not need more sugar. In an 8- or 9-inch glass pie plate, cut the margarine into 6 pieces. Microwave on **HIGH** 45 to 60 seconds until melted. Add the crumbs. Stir with a fork to coat crumbs. Press into the bottom and sides of pan. Microwave on **HIGH** 1 minute until set. Cool. Fill it with your favorite pie filling. Makes 1 pie shell.

Graham Cracker Crust

You can buy graham cracker crumbs or make your own by putting crackers in a heavy duty plastic bag and rolling with a rolling pin or bottle.

2 tbs. magarine
¾ cup graham cracker crumbs
1 tbs. sugar

Use an 8 or 9-inch microwave safe glass pie plate. Place margarine in it and microwave on **HIGH** 45 to 60 seconds until melted. Add crumbs and sugar and stir. A fork works well. Press smoothly to cover bottom and sides of pan. Microwave on **HIGH** 1 minute to set. Cool. Fill with your favorite filling. Makes 1 pie shell.

Mud Pie

This is not like the kind you made in the yard! Luckily it tastes much better, too!

1 **Cookie Crumb Crust** made with chocolate sandwich cookies (such as Oreos), page 95
½ gal. ice cream such as Cookies 'N Cream, chocolate chip or marble fudge Coffee is traditionally used, but choose whatever flavor you prefer)
Hot Fudge Sauce, page 98, cooled

Be sure the crust is cold. To soften the ice cream enough to spoon into the pie, microwave on **WARM** (10%) 3 to 5 minutes. Wait a few minutes for the temperature to equalize, and then scoop the ice cream into the crust. Cover the pie with plastic wrap and freeze for several hours or overnight.

Remove from freezer 15 minutes before serving. Top with cooled *Hot Fudge Sauce*. You could put the sauce on the ice cream before you put the pie in the freezer, but the sauce will have a gummy texture and be more difficult to cut. Makes 8 servings.

Hot Fudge Sauce

*Everyone's favorite on ice cream or cake. Use it for **Mud Pie**, page 97.*

½ cup sugar
3 tbs. cocoa
1½ tbs. cornstarch
dash salt
½ cup water
2 tbs. butter or margarine
1 tsp. vanilla

In a 2-cup glass measuring cup, mix sugar, cocoa, cornstarch and salt. Stir in water. Microwave on **HIGH** 1½ to 2 minutes, stirring every 30 seconds until almost thick. Add butter. Stir hard to melt. Stir in vanilla. Cool slightly. Makes 1 cup.

Caramel Sauce

A few tablespoons mixed with ice cream and milk makes a terrific shake.

5 tbs. butter
1 cup brown sugar
1/4 cup milk, evaporated milk, or cream
1/2 tsp. vanilla
2 tbs. white corn syrup

Combine ingredients in a 2 or 4-cup glass measuring cup. Microwave on **MEDIUM** (50%) 2 minutes, stirring every 30 seconds. Stir hard to blend after 2 minutes. This sauce thickens as it cools. It may be reheated on **MEDIUM** (50%) for about 30 to 45 seconds. Overheating will cause it to turn to sugar. Serve over ice cream or cake. Makes about 1 cup.

Praline Sauce

The famous candy from the South is changed to make a yummy topping.

½ cup milk
¼ cup light corn syrup
1 cup light brown sugar, packed
1 tbs. cornstarch
2 tbs. margarine
1 tsp. vanilla
½ cup chopped pecans

Measure milk and corn syrup into a 4-cup glass measuring cup. Place brown sugar in a small bowl. Stir in cornstarch. Add to milk. Microwave on **DEFROST** (10%) 3 to 3½ minutes, stirring after 2, until slightly thickened. Watch closely. If mixture boils to the top of the measuring cup, stop the oven and stir. Add margarine and stir to melt. Stir in vanilla and nuts. Cool slightly. Makes 1¾ cups.

Custard Sauce

Easy! Easy! Easy! The perfect topping for fruit, cake and bread pudding.

1 egg
3/4 cup milk
2 tbs. sugar
1 tsp. vanilla

Crack the egg into a 2-cup glass measuring cup. Beat with a fork. Add milk and sugar. Microwave on **MEDIUM HIGH** (70%) 3½ to 4½ minutes, stirring with the fork every minute until sauce is thick. Add vanilla. Refrigerate until cooled. Makes almost 1 cup.

Snacks and Mini Meals

The microwave is perfect for making snacks. Food can be heated or cooked in a short time. They taste good and clean up is easy. You usually don't need many ingredients, and you don't have to do much work. So these recipes are a good place to start if you are a young cook or a beginner.

Caramel Apples 103	Cheesy Crisp Chicken Bites . 112
Crunchy Crisps 104	Pita Pizza Snack 113
Finger Jello 105	Nuts and Bolts 114
S'Mores 106	Toasted Pumpkin Seeds . . 115
Soups 107	Nachos 116
Bacon Poles 108	Nachos Grande 116
Popcorn: Cheese Popcorn . . 109	Quesadillas 117
Popcorn: Nacho Popcorn . . 110	Potato Skins 118
Cheese Bites 111	

Caramel Apples

Crunchy apples covered with cream caramels satisfy any sweet tooth.

5 or 6 medium apples
5 or 6 popsicle sticks or wooden skewers
1 lb. caramels, unwrapped
1 tbs. water
chopped nuts, if you like them

Wash and dry apples well. Insert sticks through the core. Place caramels and water in a narrow deep glass bowl. Microwave on **HIGH** 2 minutes. Stir until smooth. Dip apples in caramel and twirl to coat. Dip in chopped nuts, if you like them. Place on a piece of buttered waxed paper until cool. If caramel mixture becomes too stiff to cover apples, reheat on **HIGH** 15 to 30 seconds. Makes 5 to 6 servings.

A Good Idea

For 1 apple use 9 caramels and 1 tsp. water in a cereal bowl. Microwave on **HIGH** 15 to 30 seconds just until the caramel bubbles up. Stir hard. Use a spoon to cover apple with caramel sauce.

Crunchy Crisps

Crunch, chocolate and peanut butter! Yum!

1 pkg. (6 oz.) chocolate chips (1 cup)

2 tbs. creamy peanut butter
4 rice cakes

Place chips in a small bowl. Microwave on **MEDIUM LOW** (30%) 3 minutes. Stir. Add peanut butter. Microwave on **MEDIUM HIGH** (70%) 45 seconds. Stir well to blend. Mixture should be smooth. Meanwhile, cut rice cakes in half and cut each half into 3 pieces. You will have 24 pieces. Line a pan with waxed paper. Using a butter knife, spread chocolate over each piece of rice cake. Place coated piece on waxed paper. Work very quickly, and don't lick your hands until you are finished. Place crisps in the refrigerator to harden the chocolate. Store in a cool place. Makes 24 pieces.

A Good Idea

Use a package of mini honey-nut or apple-cinnamon rice cakes. Cover the tops only with the chocolate peanut butter mixture. Refrigerate until firm.

Finger Jello

This snack will stay firm even in a lunch box.

4 cups water
3 pkg. (3 oz. each) flavored gelatin
4 envelopes (¼ oz. each) Knox plain gelatin

Measure water into an 8-cup glass measuring cup. Microwave on **HIGH** about 5 minutes until boiling. Carefully stir in gelatin and Knox gelatin until everything is dissolved. Pour into a 9 by 13-inch pan. Refrigerate until firm, several hours. Cut into small squares. Makes 40 to 50 treats.

S'Mores

So good you'll want some more.

2 graham crackers
4 small squares milk chocolate
1 large or 5 miniature marshmallows

Place 1 graham cracker square on a small plate. Cover with chocolate and then put marshmallows on chocolate. Microwave on **HIGH** 45 to 60 seconds, watching carefully as the marshmallows puff. Do not overcook. Take it out of the oven, and press the second graham cracker on top. Cool a minute before eating. Makes 1 serving.

Soups

The wide variety of canned soups available means there is something for everyone. And with a microwave oven, they are quick and easy to prepare. Beginning cooks are good cooks right now!

Start with a 4-cup glass measuring cup or a 1½-quart microwave casserole.

Water-based soups: add water according to directions. Microwave on **HIGH** 5 to 7 minutes, stirring half way and again at the end.

Cream-based soups: add milk or cream according to directions. Microwave on **MEDIUM HIGH** (70%) 7 to 8 minutes, stirring every 2 minutes. Never allow milk or cream soups to boil.

Bacon Poles

This salty crunchy snack is delicious with a mug of hot soup.

1 slice bacon
2 bread sticks
¼ cup grated Parmesan cheese

Cut a slice of bacon in half the long way. (Scissors make this easy.) Wrap a piece around each bread stick. Place the poles on 2 layers of paper towel on a plate. Cover with a second towel. Microwave on **HIGH** 1 to 1½ minutes until bacon is cooked. Remove from oven. Discard top towel. Carefully move bacon poles over to a less greasy part of the paper towel.

Meanwhile, sprinkle Parmesan cheese on another paper towel or waxed paper. Roll the pole in the cheese. Let it stand a few minutes to cool before eating. Makes 1 serving.

Popcorn: Cheese Popcorn

Popcorn is the most common microwave snack, but use only the special popcorn cooking bags or a popper designed just for the microwave. Read the instructions. **Be careful!** *Hot steam from the popcorn can be dangerous. Plain popcorn is good, and healthy, and fills you up.*

8 cups popped corn
1/4 cup butter or margarine
1/4 cup grated process cheese (like Velveeta)
1/2 cup grated Parmesan cheese
seasoned salt

Place popcorn in a 3-quart or larger bowl. In a 2-cup glass measuring cup, microwave the butter on **HIGH** 1 minute until melted. Stir in the cheeses. Drizzle over the popcorn. Toss well. Sprinkle with seasoned salt. Makes 8 cups.

Popcorn: Nacho Popcorn

If you like nacho chips you'll love nacho popcorn!

10 to 12 cups unsalted popped corn
¼ cup margarine
2 to 3 tsp. taco seasoning mix, or more for really hot flavor
½ cup shredded cheese (Monterey Jack, cheddar, Parmesan or Velveeta)

Place the popcorn in a large bowl. Place margarine in a 1-cup glass measuring cup. Microwave on **HIGH** 45 to 60 seconds until melted. Stir in taco mix. Drizzle over the popcorn. Toss lightly. Add cheese. Toss to coat. If you want to, microwave on **HIGH** about 1 minute to melt the cheese. Makes 10 to 12 cups.

Cheese Bites

A minute is all it takes to quiet the hungries. If you are a beginner, start with packaged shredded cheese.

crisp crackers (Triscuits, Wheat, Oat or Bran Thins, Cracottes)
cheese cut in ½-inch cubes or shredded cheese
garnish (sliced green onions, sliced green or black olives, sliced pepperoni, sliced mushrooms, ham cut in small pieces, salsa)

Line a plate with a paper towel or use a large heavy paper plate. Circle the plate with crackers. Top as you wish. Microwave on **HIGH:**

4 to 6 crackers	20 to 30 seconds
8 to 10 crackers	30 to 40 seconds
12 crackers	35 to 45 seconds

Watch carefully or the cheese will run all over the plate.

Cheesy Crisp Chicken Bites

My kids love these. This is good for a snack or a light supper.

3 boneless chicken breast halves, skinned
6 shredded wheat type crackers, crushed
¼ cup grated Parmesan cheese
2 tsp. dried parsley
3 tbs. butter or margarine, divided

Wash and dry the chicken. Cut each breast half into 8 pieces. Place crackers in a heavy bag and squeeze or pound to crush. Add Parmesan cheese and parsley. Mix well. Place 1 tablespoon butter in a small bowl. Microwave on **HIGH** 45 to 60 seconds to melt. Coat 8 chicken pieces with butter, then drop in bag of crumbs to coat.

Place on a microwave-safe plate or paper plate. Microwave on **HIGH** 1 to 2 minutes until chicken is cooked through and just begins to brown. Repeat with remaining chicken. Serve hot or cold. Makes 3 servings.

Pita Pizza Snack

Is there anyone in the world who doesn't love pizza? These are really easy.

2 whole wheat pitas (5-inch diameter) split in half
¼ cup pizza or spaghetti sauce
¼ cup shredded cheese
2 tbs. chopped green pepper
¼ cup sliced fresh mushrooms

Toast pita halves in a toaster. Top each with 1 tablespoon of spaghetti sauce. Add the remaining ingredients in the order listed, dividing evenly among the pitas. Place on a plate lined with a paper towel. Microwave on **HIGH** 1½ to 2½ minutes, just until cheese melts. If your microwave does not have a turntable, rotate the plate after 1 minute. Makes 4 snack servings or 2 main course servings.

A Good Idea
Add diced ham or turkey, bacon bits, chopped tomatoes or anything you like.

Nuts and Bolts

For more zip, add ½ teaspoon of chili powder and ¼ teaspoon of red pepper sauce.

½ cup (1 stick) butter or margarine
1 tbs. Worcestershire sauce
1 tsp. EACH garlic salt, onion salt, and celery salt
2 cups corn cereal
2 cups round oat cereal
2 cups Wheat Chex cereal
2 cups pretzel sticks
2 cups salted peanuts

    Place butter in a large casserole. Microwave on **HIGH** 1 minute until butter is melted. Stir in Worcestershire sauce and garlic salt. Add cereals and pretzels and toss until coated. Microwave on **HIGH** 3 minutes. Mix. Microwave on **HIGH** 2 minutes. Add peanuts and stir to mix. Allow to cool before eating or storing. Store leftovers in an airtight container. Makes 8 cups.

Toasted Pumpkin Seeds

What do you do with the seeds after you have carved your Jack-O-Lantern? Try this. It works with squash seeds, too.

1 pumpkin, top cut off
coarse (kosher) salt

Using a spoon and your hands, scoop the seeds from the pumpkin into a pan. Use clean hands to pull off the strings. Make a layer of clean seeds on a large heavy paper plate. Use a second plate if you need it.

Sprinkle with salt. For each plate, microwave on **HIGH** 1 minute. Stir with a fork or spoon. Microwave on **HIGH** 30 seconds more; stir. Continue to microwave on **HIGH** 1 to 2 minutes, stirring every 30 seconds until seeds are crisp and dry. Add a little more salt if needed. Cool. Store in an airtight container.

Nachos

This is a big favorite with lots of kids of all ages! Use any cheese you like.

1 pkg. (7½ oz.) tortilla corn chips
1 cup (4 oz.) grated cheese

2 tbs. sliced green chiles
chili salsa

Cover a paper plate with chips in a single layer. Sprinkle cheese over chips. Top with chiles if desired. Microwave on **MEDIUM HIGH** (70%) 1 to 1½ minutes just until cheese melts. Dot with salsa. Makes 1 serving.

Nachos Grande

1 can (15½ oz.) refried beans
1 pkg. (14 oz.) tortilla corn chips
1½ cups grated cheddar cheese
olives, thinly sliced

jalapeño peppers, thinly sliced
2 tbs. chopped green chiles
¼ cup sliced green onions

Spread 1 tsp. beans on each of 8 chips. Arrange in a circle on a paper plate or towel. Top each with cheese and remaining ingredients. Microwave on **HIGH** 20 to 40 seconds until cheese melts. Repeat. Makes about 4 to 6 servings.

Quesadillas

Say it: kay-sah-dee-yahs. Try quesadillas for a quick after-school snack.

2 flour tortillas
½ cup grated cheese

chopped green chiles, if you like them
salsa or taco sauce, if you like it

Place 1 tortilla on a paper towel-lined plate or paper plate. Sprinkle cheese on top, spreading to ¼-inch from the edge. Add chiles if you want a hotter snack. Microwave on **HIGH** 40 to 60 seconds just until you see the cheese melt. Remove from oven and press the second tortilla on the cheese. Remove the paper towel and turn the quesadilla over. Cut into 8 pieces. Clean scissors work well. Dip in salsa or taco sauce if you wish. Makes 1 serving.

SNACKS AND MINI MEALS

Potato Skins

This is a favorite order when you go to a restaurant, and now you can make it at home, easily.

3 medium potatoes, baked (see directions, page 80)
1 tbs. margarine
¼ tsp. dried dill weed
dash of hot pepper sauce
dash of garlic salt
¾ cup (3 oz.) shredded Swiss cheese
3 green onions, sliced, including some green part

Wrap baked potatoes in a kitchen towel for 15 minutes. When cool enough to handle, cut in half. Remove all but ¼ inch of the potato flesh and save this for another purpose. Place margarine in a small microwave-safe dish and microwave on **HIGH** about 45 seconds to melt. Stir in dill weed, pepper and garlic salt. Brush on both sides of potato skins.

Arrange in a circle on a heavy paper plate or 2 paper towels with cut sides of potato down. Microwave on **HIGH** 6 to 7 minutes. Turn over. Divide cheese among the potatoes. Sprinkle with green onions. Microwave on **HIGH** 1 minute until cheese melts. Makes 6 servings.

Candy

Homemade candy makes a special gift, or a delicious treat. Usually only a few ingredients are needed. Measuring is easy. Cooking time is very short. All of this means that making candy is perfect if you are a beginner.

No Bake Chews	120	**Peanut Brittle**	128
Quickie Fudge	121	**Caramels**	129
Popcorn Wreath	122	**Taffy**	130
Almond Bark	124	**Peter Pans**	131
Mints	125	**Peanut Butter Flakes**	132
Chocolate Nests with Eggs	126	**Rice Krispies Treats**	133
English Toffee	127	**Scotch Krispies**	134

No Bake Chews

*Chocolate chips hold their shape even when microwaved. It is important to stir to help them melt smoothly. These are **super** easy.*

1 pkg. (6 oz.) butterscotch chips
1 pkg. (6 oz.) chocolate chips
1 can (3 oz.) chow mein noodles
1 cup raisins or miniature marshmallows

Place butterscotch and chocolate chips in a 2-quart casserole. Microwave on **MEDIUM** (50%) 4 to 5 minutes. Stir after 3 minutes and every minute after until all the chips are melted. Stir hard until the mixture is smooth. Stir in the noodles and the raisins or marshmallows. Drop spoonfuls of the mixture onto a cookie sheet lined with waxed paper. Put the cookie sheet into the refrigerator for an hour or until the candies are firm. Makes 40 to 48 pieces.

Quickie Fudge

The fastest and easiest way to have some chocolate when you really want it!

1 lb. powdered sugar
½ cup cocoa
¼ cup milk, cream or half-and-half
8 tbs. (1 stick) margarine or butter
1 tbs. vanilla
½ cup chopped nuts

In a microwave-safe bowl, blend the sugar and cocoa. Add milk and margarine without mixing. Microwave on **HIGH** 2 minutes. Stir hard until just mixed. Add the vanilla and nuts and stir well. Pour the mixture into a greased 8 or 9-inch square or round pan. Place in the freezer for 20 minutes or refrigerator for 1 hour to harden. Cut into small squares. Makes 16 squares or 60 small bites, 1½ pounds.

Popcorn Wreath

Your wreath can last up to 2 weeks if you can keep people from eating it.

8 cups popped salt-free microwave popcorn
½ cup butter or margarine
½ cup sugar
8 large or 1 cup miniature marshmallows
4 to 5 drops green food color (if you want it)
candy for decorating: red gum drops, red jelly beans, green leaf-shaped gumdrops

Cover a cookie sheet with waxed paper. Put popped corn in a large bowl. Measure butter, sugar and marshmallows into an 8-cup glass measuring cup. Microwave on **HIGH** 4 to 5 minutes, stirring 2 times, until marshmallows are melted. *Very carefully* stir in a tiny amount of food color. (If you should spill, wipe up quickly with a wet paper towel.)

Pour the melted marshmallow over the popcorn, and toss it with a large spoon. Touch it carefully. Is it cool enough? If it is, use your hands to drop the mixture on the waxed paper, pushing it into a ring or wreath shape. Decorate the wreath with candies. Let it stand 30 minutes until it is set. Finish the wreath with a bow, if you want to. Store it in a cool dry place, loosely covered with plastic wrap. Makes one 12-ounce wreath.

Almond Bark

If time is short and you are hungry, think of almond bark. You only need 3 ingredients, 10 minutes, and a short time to chill the candy.

1 cup slivered almonds
1 tsp. butter or oil
16 oz. white chocolate, broken into pieces

Place the almonds and butter in a 9-inch glass pie pan. Microwave on **HIGH** 4½ to 5½ minutes, stirring 2 or 3 times, until toasted. Cool. Cover a baking sheet with waxed paper. Place the chocolate in a glass mixing bowl. Microwave on **HIGH** 2 minutes. Stir. If all of the mixture is not soft, microwave on **HIGH** 1 to 1½ minutes longer. Stir in almonds. Pour onto waxed paper, and spread it out until it is about ¼-inch thick. Refrigerate about 1 hour until the candy is firm. Break it into pieces. Makes 1¼ pounds.

Mints

A plate of mints makes a special gift for a teacher or Grandma.

6 oz. cream cheese
1 lb. powdered sugar, sifted
1 tsp. flavoring (wintergreen, mint or peppermint)
1 tiny drop green or red food coloring

Unwrap cream cheese and place it in a glass bowl. Microwave on **MEDIUM HIGH** (70%) for 1 to 1½ minutes until soft. Add remaining ingredients. Stir very well. Drop by teaspoonfuls onto waxed paper. Using a fork, press a ridged pattern into the top of each mint. Makes about 1¼ pounds.

Chocolate Nests with Eggs

Nests can be wrapped in waxed paper or plastic wrap and refrigerated for storage.

1 bar (7 oz.) milk chocolate
1 pkg. (4 oz.) sweet baking chocolate
1 pkg. (4 oz.) shredded coconut
2 cups crushed cornflakes
jelly beans in several colors

Cover baking sheet with waxed paper. Place chocolates in a 2-quart casserole. Microwave on **HIGH** 2 to 3 minutes until melted. Stir until smooth. Stir in coconut and cornflakes. Drop by large spoonfuls onto waxed paper. Using your hands, shape each spoonful into a nest shape. Decorate with 4 jelly beans. Refrigerate until firm. Makes 20 nests.

English Toffee

An all-time favorite of everyone.

3/4 cup butter
1 cup firmly packed brown sugar

3/4 cup finely chopped almonds, divided
1/2 cup semisweet chocolate chips

    Line an 8-inch square pan with foil. Spray with nonstick cooking spray or wipe with butter. Set aside. In an 8-quart glass measuring cup, place butter and sugar. Microwave, uncovered, on **HIGH** 1 minute. Bet with a wire whisk until smooth. Microwave on **HIGH** 4 minutes. Stir in 1/2 cup almonds. Microwave on **HIGH 2** minutes until mixture thickens. Watch carefully as sugar burns quickly. Stir with a wire whisk.
    Put the prepared pan on a flat surface; pour into the pan. Sprinkle with chocolate chips. Cover with plastic wrap for 3 to 4 minutes to melt the chocolate. Carefully spread it over the candy. Immediately sprinkle with remaining nuts. Refrigerate until the chocolate hardens. Remove from pan. Peel off the foil. Break into small pieces. Pack in an airtight container and refrigerate. Makes about 1 pound.

Peanut Brittle

The chemical reaction between the syrup and the baking soda is fun to watch.

1 cup Spanish peanuts
1 cup sugar
½ cup light corn syrup
½ tsp. salt
1 tsp. vanilla
1 tsp. margarine
1 tsp. baking soda

Grease a baking sheet and set it aside. In a 1½-quart casserole, stir together the peanuts, sugar, corn syrup and salt. Microwave on **HIGH** 7 to 8 minutes, stirring after 4 minutes. Add vanilla and margarine, and stir it together well. Microwave on **HIGH** 1 to 2 minutes. Peanuts will brown lightly and syrup will be very hot. Be careful! Add soda and stir gently until light and foamy. Pour the syrup onto the cookie sheet. Cool ½ to 1 hour. Break into pieces. Store in an airtight container. Makes about 1 pound.

Caramels

It wouldn't be Christmas without caramels. They make a wonderful gift, too. You will need a special microwave candy thermometer, and adult help is advised, but the wrapping is fun for young hands.

1 cup butter
2 cups sugar
2 cups light corn syrup
2 cups (1 pint) whipping cream
1 tbs. vanilla

Butter a 9- by 13-inch pan and set aside. Place butter in a 4-quart glass bowl. Microwave on **HIGH** 1 to 1½ minutes, uncovered, until melted. Stir in sugar, corn syrup and 1 cup cream. Microwave on **HIGH** 24 minutes, uncovered. Insert microwave candy thermometer. Microwave on **HIGH** 12 to 14 minutes until mixture reaches 245° (firm ball) stage). Stir in vanilla. Pour into buttered pan. Chill overnight. Cut into small squares. Wrap in waxed paper or plastic wrap. Store in cool place. Makes 96 pieces.

Taffy

Ask your mom or grandmother if they remember having taffy pulls. Bet they do!

2 cups sugar
¼ cup white vinegar
¼ cup water
1 tsp. vanilla

Mix sugar, vinegar and water in an 8-cup glass measuring cup. Microwave on **HIGH** 6 minutes, stirring every 2 minutes. Continue to cook without stirring on **HIGH** for 3 to 4 minutes, until a candy thermometer reads 280°. Pour out onto two large plates.

When cool enough to handle, use your hands to work in the vanilla. Then, with a friend, begin to pull taffy until it turns shiny white. Continue stretching, pulling and twisting like a rope. Snip into bite-sized pieces with scissors. This takes some practice, so be patient. It helps to put butter on your hands so the candy won't stick to them.

Peter Pans

These instant candy squares have all your favorite flavors.

1 pkg. (6 oz.) chocolate chips
1 pkg. (6 oz.) butterscotch chips
½ cup margarine
¾ cup peanut butter
2 cups miniature marshmallows
6 oz. salted peanuts

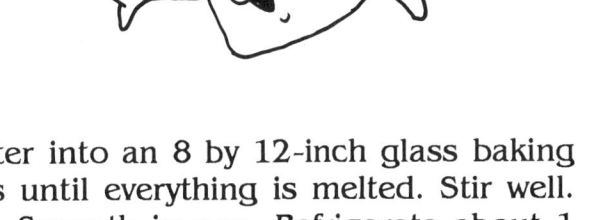

Place chips, margarine and peanut butter into an 8 by 12-inch glass baking pan. Microwave on **HIGH** 2 to 3 minutes until everything is melted. Stir well. Cool. Stir in marshmallows and peanuts. Smooth in pan. Refrigerate about 1 hour. When firm, cut into small squares. Makes about 48.

Peanut Butter Flakes

Very young children can use their hands to help form these cereal snacks.

1 cup sugar
1 cup light corn syrup
1 cup creamy or crunchy peanut butter
6 to 8 cups cornflakes

Cover a baking sheet with waxed paper. In an 8-cup glass measuring cup, stir together sugar, syrup and peanut butter. Microwave on **HIGH** 6 minutes, stirring after 3. Stir again after 6 minutes. Add cornflakes and stir well. Drop onto waxed paper or mold with hands. Refrigerate to set. Makes 48 pieces.

Rice Krispies Treats

This recipe has stood the test of time. Your grandma probably made it years ago.

¼ cup butter or margarine
45 large marshmallows or 4 cups
  miniature marshmallows
5 cups crisp rice cereal

Place butter and marshmallows in a 3-quart casserole. Microwave on HIGH 3 minutes, stirring every minute. Add cereal and mix until completely covered. Press into an 8 by 12-inch glass pan. Chill. Cut into bars. Makes 24 bars.

Scotch Krispies

Three ingredients and a few minutes and you have delicious candy.

½ cup peanut butter
1 pkg. (6 oz.) butterscotch bits
3 cups crisp rice cereal

Cover a baking sheet with waxed paper. In an 8-cup glass measure, place peanut butter and butterscotch bits. Microwave on **HIGH** 4 to 5 minutes. Stir until smooth. Add cereal and stir until it is coated with the mixture. Drop by spoonfuls onto waxed paper. Chill until firm. Makes 24 pieces.

Index

Acorn squash 69
Almond bark 124
Apple upside-down cake 92
Appleberry salad 32
Apples, baked 33
Applesauce 36

Bacon 22
Bacon poles 108
Baked apples 33
Beef taco casserole 61
Blueberry coffee cake 24
Bread pudding 89
Breakfast 19-28
    bacon 22
    blueberry coffee cake 24
    eggs in a blanket 23
    green eggs and ham 21
    huevos rancheros 23
    old-fashioned oatmeal 25
    quick muffins 28
    quick oatmeal 25
    refrigerator bran muffins 26
    scrambled eggs 20

Cake
    apple upside-down 92
Candy 119-134
    almond bark 124
    caramels 129
    chocolate nests with eggs 126
    English toffee 127
    mints 125
    no bake chews 120
    peanut brittle 128
    peanut butter flakes 132
    peter pans 131
    popcorn wreath 122
    quickie fudge 121
    rice krispies treats 133
    Scotch krispies 134
    taffy 130
Caramel
    apples 103
    sauce 99
Caramels 129
Casseroles 53-67
    beef taco casserole 61
    chicken 65
    chicken enchiladas 62
    chopstick tuna 59
    easy lasagna 56
    hamburger Stroganoff 55
    lasagna whirls 58
    macaroni and cheese 66
    Sunday night supper 63
    tuna macaroni 64
    tuna noodle casserole 60
Cheese
    bites 111
    popcorn 109
    sandwich 48
Cheesy crisp chicken bites 112
Chicken
    bites, cheesy crisp 112
    casserole 65
    enchilladas 62
    saucy 43
Chocolate
    nests with eggs 126
    pudding 86
Chopstick tuna 59
Cocoa from a mix 14

Cookie crumb crust 95
Corn
   on the cob 71
   pudding 72
Crunchy crisps 104
Custard sauce 101

Desserts 85-101
   apple upside-down cake 92
   bread pudding 89
   caramel sauce 99
   cookie crumb crust 95
   custard sauce 101
   frosty lemon pie 94
   ginger spice bars 90
   graham cracker crust 96
   hot fudge sauce 98
   lemon icing 91
   mud pie 97
   one-dish brownies 93
   pb and j pudding 87
   plum good bars 88
   praline sauce 100

strawberry pretzel 38
vanilla pudding 86

Easy
   lasagna 56
   spaghetti 47
Eggs in a blanket 23
English toffee 127
Equivalents in microwave times 10

Finger jello 105
Fish
   chopstick tuna 59
   oven baked 42
   tuna melt 52
   tuna noodle casserole 60
   tuna 'taters 83
   tunaburgers 51
Frosty lemon pie 94
Frozen banana pops 31
Fruits 30-40
   appleberry salad 32
   applesauce 36

baked apples 33
frozen banana pops 31
peach cobbler 35
pear crisp 40
poached pears 34
strawberry pretzel dessert 38

Ginger spice bars 90
Glossary 11
Graham cracker crust 96
Green bean bake 73
Green eggs and ham 21

Hamburger Stroganoff 55
Hot dogs and buns 49
Hot drinks 12-18
   cocoa from a mix 14
   hot lemon tea 15
   hot vegetable cocktail 17
   Nanny's cocoa mix 14

old-fashioned cocoa 13
orange spiced tea 16
spiced cider 18
Hot fudge sauce 98
Hot lemon tea 15
Hot vegetable cocktail 17
Huevos rancheros 23

Lasagna
   easy 56
   whirls 58
Lemon icing 91

Macaroni and cheese 66
Main course 41-52
   cheese sandwich 48
   easy spaghetti 47
   hot dogs and buns 49
   oven baked fish 42
   pizza fondue 46
   saucy chicken 43
   sloppy Joes 50
   tuna melt 52

tunaburgers 51
turkey loaf 45
turkey Parmesan 44
Microwave
   how it operates 9
Mints 125
Morris's favorite 'tater topping 84
Mud pie 97
Muffins
   pan, about 29
   quick 28
   refrigerator bran 26
   timings 27

Nacho popcorn 110
Nachos 116
Nachos grande 116
Nanny's cocoa mix 14
No bake chews 120
Note to kids 6
Note to parents 1
Nuts and bolts 114

Oatmeal
   old-fashioned 25
   quick 25

Old-fashioned cocoa 13
Old-fashioned oatmeal 25
One-dish brownies 93
Orange
   glazed carrots 70
   scalloped sweet potatoes 77
   spiced tea 16
Oven baked fish 42

Pb and j pudding 87
Peach cobbler 35
Peanut brittle 128
Peanut butter flakes 132
Pear crisp 40
Peter pans 131
Pie
   cookie crumb crust 95
   frosty lemon 94
   graham cracker crust 96
   mud 97
Pita pizza snack 113
Pizza fondue 46
Plum good bars 88

Poached pears 34
Popcorn
   cheese 109
   nacho 110
   wreath 122
Potato skins 118
Potatoes, baked 80
Praline sauce 100
Pudding
   bread 89
   chocolate 86
   pb and j 87
   vanilla 86

Quesadillas 117
Quick muffins 28
Quick oatmeal 25
Quickie fudge 121

Refrigerator bran muffins 26
Rice krispies treats 133

S'mores 106
Safety test 3
Safety tips 2

Sauce
   caramel 99
   custard 101
   hot fudge 98
   praline sauce 100
Saucy chicken 43
Scotch krispies 134
Scrambled eggs 20
Sloppy Joes 50
Snacks 102-118
   bacon poles 108
   caramel apples 103
   cheese bites 111
   cheese popcorn 109
   cheesy crisp chicken bites 112
   crunchy crisps 104
   finger jello 105
   nacho popcorn 110
   nachos 116
   nachos grande 116
   nuts and bolts 114
   pita pizza snack 113
   potato skins 118
   quesadillas 117
   s'mores 106
   soups 107

toasted pumpkin seeds 115
Soups 107
Spaghetti, easy 47
Spiced cider 18
Strawberry pretzel dessert 38
Sunday night supper 63
Sweet potatoes, orange scalloped 77

Taffy 130
'Taters
   Morris's favorite topping 84
   other toppings 84
   tacos 82
   tuna 83
   with cheese sauce 81
Toasted pumpkin seeds 115
Tomato zucchini dish 76
Tuna
   chopstick 59
   macaroni casserole 64
   melt 52

noodle casserole 60
'taters 83
burgers 51
Turkey
   loaf 45
   Parmesan 44

Vanilla pudding 86
Veggie bobs 74
Veggies 68-84
   acorn squash 69
   baked potatoes 80
   bobs 74
   corn on the cob 71
   corn pudding 72
   fresh yams 79
   green bean bake 73
   Morris's favorite 'tater topping 84
   orange glazed carrots 70
   orange scalloped sweet potatoes 77
   'tater tacos 82
   'tater toppings 81-84
   'taters with cheese sauce 81

tomato zucchini dish 76
tuna 'taters 83
yam and apple casserole 78
Yam(s)
   and apple casserole 78
   fresh 79

SERVE CREATIVE, EASY, NUTRITIOUS MEALS — COLLECT THEM ALL

The Kid's Microwave Cookbook
The Bread Machine Cookbook
Microwave Cooking for 1 or 2
Recipes for the 9x13 Pan
Turkey, The Magic Ingredient
Chocolate Cherry Tortes and Other Lowfat Delights
Lowfat American Favorites
Lowfat International Cuisine
The Hunk Cookbook
Now That's Italian!
Fabulous Fiber Cookery
Low Salt, Low Sugar, Low Fat Desserts
What's for Breakfast?
Healthy Cooking on the Run
Healthy Snacks for Kids
Creative Soups & Salads
Quick & Easy Pasta Recipes
Muffins, Nut Breads and More
The Barbecue Book
The Wok
New Ways with Your Wok

Quiche & Soufflé Cookbook
Easy Microwave Cooking
Compleat American Housewife 1787
Cooking for 1 or 2
Brunch
Cocktails & Hors d'Oeuvres
Meals in Minutes
New Ways to Enjoy Chicken
Favorite Seafood Recipes
No Salt, No Sugar, No Fat Cookbook
The Fresh Vegetable Cookbook
Modern Ice Cream Recipes
Crepes & Omelets
Time-Saving Gourmet Cooking
New International Fondue Cookbook
Extra-Special Crockery Pot Recipes
Favorite Cookie Recipes
Authentic Mexican Cooking
Fisherman's Wharf Cookbook
The Kid's Cookbook
The Best of Nitty Gritty
The Creative Lunch Box

Write or call for our free catalog.
Bristol Publishing Enterprises, Inc.
P.O. Box 1737, San Leandro, CA 94577
(800)346-4889 or (415)895-4461